FALLEN ANGEL
SINNERS AND ANGELS DUET BOOK TWO

TESSA JAMES

fallen ANGEL

TESSA JAMES

Copyright © 2021 by Tessa James

All rights reserved.

No part of this book may be reproduced in any form or by any electronic or mechanical means, including information storage and retrieval systems, without written permission from the author, except for the use of brief quotations in a book review.

This is a work of fiction. Names, characters, places, and incidents either are the product of the author's imagination or are used fictitiously. Any resemblance to actual persons, living or dead, events, or locales is entirely coincidental.

Book Cover Design by https://trcdesigns.ca
Photography by https://www.thetalknerdy.com
Editing by https://librumartis.com
First Edition 2021
ISBN 978-1-7332322-9-6 *(paperback)*
ASIN B096BLM4WJ *(ebook)*

This one is dedicated to my best friend—coffee. Because without it, all of those late nights and early mornings spent writing this book would have been a heck of a lot more difficult.

JOHNNY – 1

I shouldn't be alive.

But for whatever fucking miracle, I am.

At one point, I truly believed I was dying. And that memory will forever be burned into my mind.

Claire held me in her arms, sobs rippling through her. I couldn't get the bleeding to stop, and despite the pain and numbness taking turns assaulting me, the only thing I could think about was leaving her behind.

That alone killed me in its own way.

In what I thought was my final moment, I uttered the words I needed her to hear.

That I loved her.

It wasn't really how I planned her birthday to go, but there was no way I was going to depart from this world without making sure she knew how I felt.

Luckily, our story didn't end there.

At least for us, it didn't. To almost everyone on the West Coast, I died in the street that brisk fall evening, in front of Bram's diner.

Tragically, poetically, and randomly.

I'd be lying if I said a part of that wasn't true. Because I did die that day. Claire and I both did. A traumatic situation will do that to a person. Break you down and mold you into another version of yourself. A darker one. One that you cannot come back from.

My shooter was never found.

The cops chalked it up to a robbery gone wrong, but there's no denying it was Franklin's doing.

From the moment I stepped foot into Franklin's world, he had been searching for a way to get rid of me. He knew I wasn't like the others. That I wasn't corruptible enough to turn into the minion he expected of me. I was obedient, but only to an extent. My goal was always to free Billy from his grasp and then make my own way out.

I was good, he was evil.

And he knew it.

The only way to ensure I would no longer do his business any damage was to take me out completely. He started with Steve and Jared—staging their double homicide—and followed it up with my incident. Franklin cleaned his slate of the mess I made and didn't blink twice about the casualties that piled up in his wake.

Franklin is cruel and ruthless.

Getting away from him was my only chance of survival, especially now that Claire's involved. I couldn't risk putting her in any more danger than I already had. If anything, Franklin did me a huge fucking favor by setting the first piece in place.

I had been struggling to figure out how to make a proper exit from his clutches, and aside from it nearly killing me, it was the exact thing I needed to set everything in motion.

I put that life behind me the second the opportunity presented itself.

Josey crosses my mind from time to time. I wish I could have told him the truth. That I didn't actually meet my demise that day. But if I had, it could have ruined the whole plan. I needed him to believe I was dead if I wanted Franklin to buy the story, too. Josey had been such a brother to me, but I couldn't take that risk with the odds already stacked against me.

Claire played her part well, convincing everyone around her that she was grieving the loss of her boyfriend. I don't entirely buy that her performance was fabricated, given how emotional she was throughout the entire thing. I can only imagine how horrible it was to witness everything play out from her point of view. It was as though she bottled her anger and rage toward Franklin and channeled it into what everyone saw on the outside.

Hell, she even smacked Josey, which only made the entire thing that much more realistic.

"Hey," Claire calls out from the entrance of the bathroom.

My heart skips a beat, reminding me I am very much alive, and she is still an angel gracing me with her presence.

A towel clings to her wet body, and her dark hair cascades down both sides of her beautiful face.

"Hi." I sit on our new couch in complete and utter awe of her. It's like no matter how much time passes, I still can't believe she picked me. After everything we've been through, she's here.

It's been a rocky road, but we've traversed it together.

Claire's already flushed from the shower cheeks redden even more. She shakes her head. "We're already late, don't even think about it."

I grin and run my hand along my scalp, the hair prickling my fingertips. I haven't quite gotten used to the fact that my hair is short now. A potentially necessary change given the circumstances. "Come on, what's another fifteen minutes?"

She ruffles her head with a towel. "That's what you said earlier. I have to draw the line somewhere." Claire smiles and continues. "We won't be gone long. Just enough to watch the ball drop and do the *happy New Year* crap."

"You sure it's a good idea?"

"Rose said it's low-key. Her and a few friends. Remember Holland and Pax? They'll be there. We have to practice being *normal* if we're ever going to properly return to society."

She's not wrong. We've been here almost two months and we only leave the apartment when it's necessary. I keep waiting for something to go wrong. A sign that our plan failed, that Franklin found us and he's going to finish what he started. But weeks have gone by, and nothing has happened. Life really has been relatively mundane. So much so that Claire starts her second semester of college in a few days.

"No social media?" I ask her. It was something we agreed to when forming our escape plan. I can't risk my face accidentally being in a frame and Franklin finding out I'm still alive.

"Nope. There's a strict phone in bowl policy when you walk in the door thing going on."

Claire's longtime best friend, Rosey, is mostly on a need-to-know basis for our unusual situation. She was the only person on the East Coast that knew of my existence, and considering her role in Claire's life, we had to come up with something. To her, I'm Johnny, but to everyone else here, I'm Theo.

Coined from my middle name, compliments of Claire.

It complicates things, but it's better than the alternative. I couldn't be Johnny anymore, at least not to the public eye. Not until I knew for sure that we were safe, and Franklin was a person from our past.

Although, I have no idea how or even if that will ever be possible.

He's a powerful man and will stop at nothing to fulfill his twisted desires.

"Did you get the mail earlier?" Claire snaps me out of my trance.

I plant my hands on my thighs and stand from the couch. "Nope. But I will now." I glance at my watch. "You better hurry."

"Thanks, babe." Claire goes back into the bathroom.

We've gotten into the habit of using cheesy pet names because it's much easier to remember than my own. There have been a few times she's slipped up and called me Johnny, but it's managed to go unnoticed by outsiders.

It's not ideal, to live this hidden life, but it's what makes sense for now until the dust has settled. I haven't even fully recovered from the gunshot wound and the surgery that followed, let alone mentally prepare for a war against Franklin if he manages to find out I duped him.

Claire has already sacrificed so much to be with me; I owe it to her to play along and attempt to bring some level of normalcy back to our lives.

I step into the crisp air and instantly regret not grabbing my jacket on the way out. The mailboxes aren't too far of a walk, but considering I was born and raised out west, I've never really known a true winter. I actually hadn't seen snow in person until a few weeks ago. It's sort of mesmerizing to witness, each little flake gently sprinkling down from the sky and slowly accumulating into a frigid, white wonderland.

My body shivers and each breath spouts out another small, misty cloud as my boots slosh through the mess of slush in front of the large community mailbox. Between the mail-forwarding service and the winter storm we had last Monday, mail has been running slower than usual. I slide our key into our lock and pull out the stacks of envelopes. I thumb through them, looking for the one Claire is anxious to receive.

Her scholarship information.

The financial aspect of our relocation has been difficult for her to process. Despite reassuring her that I can cover all of our expenses, she's still adamant about making sure the funds go through. Even after all of our moving costs, I could still pay her tuition ten times over if I needed to. Getting her to understand that, though, is a challenge in itself.

I assume part of it is because she's fiercely independent. She doesn't want to have to rely on someone else. Claire prefers to pull her own weight and handle things on her own. And honestly, I admire that about her. That she's ambitious and self-sufficient—fully capable of handling pretty much whatever is thrown her way.

She's a badass, really.

But we're in this together, and I would have never made it this far without her. Pitching in and helping monetarily is the very least I could do. I owe her my life.

A slip of paper tucked between our water bill and a piece of spam mail catches my eye. There is no stamp, no return address, just a folded white sheet. I glance over my shoulder, the weight of eyes suddenly on me despite being completely alone.

I should crumple it up, toss it in the recycling and not give it another thought.

Instead, I do the thing that I somehow know with certainty is going to change everything.

I open it up.

Red ink stares back at me, probably chosen for its dramatic effect.

Scrawled across the page are the words: *Thought you could hide from me?*

Suddenly, I'm not cold anymore.

My jaw tenses, and I clench the note in my fist. This is exactly what I had been worried about all these weeks, and part of me thought that maybe I had fooled him. That I had escaped his deadly grip.

Fear washes over me and my attention settles on our little apartment up ahead, with the one person who means the most to me tucked inside.

I slide my phone out of my pocket and scroll until I find the number I'm looking for. I scan the texts, noting the last few responses.

Since I've been on the east coast, I've maintained one trusted contact back home. Someone to keep an eye on Franklin in case he leaves. He has many people working for him, but at this point, I think I've pissed him off enough that he would finish the job himself if given the chance. And that's why I keep tabs on his whereabouts, in case I need to make a move of my own.

His note could mean several things. It's possible that he only got wind of our relationship, and has decided to evoke a little fear in her to see if it can flush me out, to prove whether or not I survived his attack. Or, he very well could know the truth of the situation and this could have been meant for me. He's such a sick fuck that there's a chance he could believe I'm dead but somehow *still* want to ruin me even after I'm gone.

Whatever his intentions, he's aware of Claire's whereabouts, and that alone is a big issue.

Tomorrow, I will start looking for another apartment, I'll switch our mail over to a post office box, and I'll do everything I can to ensure Claire's safety while allowing her to somewhat get back to her life. The cold air cools my raging nerves as I shove the message into my pocket and walk toward our apparently very temporary home.

"Anything important?" Claire asks me once I'm inside. She's changed into a dark green oversized sweater and black leggings. I swear that girl would look sexy wearing a paper bag.

I swallow down the truth and greet her with a lie. "Just some bills."

Her face drops and she nods. "Maybe this week."

I cross the space between us and tip her chin up to look at me. "It's going to come, okay? And even if it doesn't, we're going to be fine. No matter what happens."

She bites at her lip. "Yeah."

"We're stuck with each other, remember?" Using the words she's used on me many times, I wink at her. I still have no fucking clue how I got lucky enough to be with Claire, but I treat each day as a blessing—especially considering my close call with death, an experience I hope I don't have to do again for a very long time.

Claire stands on her tiptoes and presses her lips gently to mine. "Good."

Every kiss feels like the first with her, sending a swarm of butterflies through me. I keep wondering if that will ever go away, but with her, I wouldn't be surprised if it lasts forever.

My only hope is that she experiences it, too.

The love and happiness she brings me is what keeps me going. What makes me believe that despite our fucked-up situation, as long as we're together, we'll be fine.

Even with the looming note burning a hole in my pocket.

We will make it through.

CLAIRE – 2

ALMOST TWO MONTHS AGO

I've never been in more pain in my entire life.

My heart rips wide open watching the light leave Johnny's eyes and the blood pool around our bodies.

I scream for help, but I don't think anyone hears me.

I hold his body to my chest, begging him not to go. His last three words are a twisted lullaby I will never forget. If only there was a way to change places with him. To sacrifice myself instead of him. I'd give anything, do anything, to give him a second chance at life.

Hands find my shoulders. Large ones. They threaten to tear me away from him, but I won't go. I can't. Not yet.

"Claire." Bram's voice finally comes through. He's frantic, for obvious reasons. He kneels next to us and applies pressure to Johnny's seeping wound. "Help is on the way."

I don't dare look up at Bram. If I take my eyes off Johnny, he might disappear forever.

Sirens appear in the distance and grow louder with their approach.

Tears roll down my cheek and onto the only man I've ever truly fallen in love with.

In a few months' time, Johnny had shown me more kindness and compassion than I thought possible. He respected me and taught me what love between two people was actually supposed to feel like. In a way, he repaired the damage done by my past with each gentle and thoughtful thing he had done. He gave me hope that the world wasn't really a terrible place like it seemed.

But watching such a terrible thing happen to such a great person, I'm not so sure anymore.

Johnny didn't deserve this.

After everything he's given up, his story should not have ended here.

How am I supposed to go on without him?

"Clear the way!" someone shouts.

A moment later, paramedics are in front of me. "What happened?"

Bram speaks up. "Gunshot wound to the abdomen."

"Ma'am, we're going to need you to let go."

I blink and Johnny is out of my grasp, lying on a stretcher, blood all over him. I reach out like I can somehow magnetically bring him back to me.

They do their work on the move, taking him further and further away from me.

I snap out of my shock and hop up from the dirty ground, rushing behind them.

An older man holds his arm out. "Family only."

Shock rattles my core. They didn't seem to care when it was Griffin; why do they all of a sudden have rules now?"

"I—I." My mouth seems to fail at forming a sentence.

"She is family," Bram says from beside me.

When did he get there?

"Are you his father?" asks the medic while climbing into the big flashing vehicle.

"No, but she—"

The guy cuts Bram off by slamming the door shut.

The air leaves my chest, and I find myself unable to breathe. "No," is all I manage to get out. This can't be it. He can't be gone.

I take off toward the medic, my arm extended to grab onto the door latch. I can't let them take him from me.

The brake lights illuminate, and it lurches away from me.

I call out, this time louder. "No, wait!"

Bram grabs me by the shoulders. "Come on, I'll drive." He turns me toward the entrance of the diner, where people are scattered about, staring at us.

I follow him over to the old truck and hop into the passenger seat without another thought. Once inside, I feel the invisible thread connecting me and Johnny being pulled apart.

I desperately bite at the inside of my cheek to stop the overwhelming wave of emotions threatening to completely ruin me.

Bram wastes no time turning over the engine and rushing out of the parking spot to catch up to the ambulance. The tires squeal, but he isn't bothered. He blows through a red light and cuts through traffic to place us right behind them.

A few agonizing minutes later, we pull up to the emergency room, where Johnny is carted out of the back and brought into the hospital. I barely wait for Bram to stop his truck before I jump out and rush toward them.

Bram is at my side within seconds.

Machines beep. Automatic doors open. Other people in the medical field come rushing over to ask questions and start their assessment.

"Caucasian male, approximately twenty years old, gunshot wound. BP dropping."

I get stopped by two women in front of a set of doors. "You can't go back there."

I stand tall to glance through the small window and note the words *surgery* and *critical condition* that float back to me.

"Where are they taking him?" I blurt out.

The lady in the obnoxiously bright polka-dot-covered

scrubs says, "You can wait in the third-floor waiting room." She points across the way. "Elevator is to your left up ahead."

Bram places his hand on my back and leads me toward it without saying a word.

We rush over, despite knowing we have a long road ahead of us until we get any news on Johnny's condition.

I cling to the little bit of hope that he will make it through this. He has to.

We step into the elevator and an elderly woman holding herself up with a cane stares at us.

I go to the opposite side and glance down at my body. I'm covered in Johnny's blood and I can feel the hair that is matted to my cheeks from my tears. To her, I probably look like I just stepped out of a horror movie scene.

Bram and I get off at three and go into the empty waiting room.

"They're not going to tell us anything." I settle into a seat in the corner and pick at my thumb. I turn to him and finally meet his gaze. "Will you say you're his dad? Please?" I barely get the words out without choking on the sob that bubbles up.

Bram nods without hesitation. "Absolutely."

The tiniest bit of relief washes over me. It's not much, but at least now we won't completely be in the dark with what's going on with Johnny.

"Claire," Bram speaks quietly. "This wasn't an accident, was it?"

I clench my jaw. Johnny has done what he could to make sure Bram was left out of this side of Johnny's world, but now, how can I lie to him given the circumstances? Doesn't Bram deserve to know a portion of the truth?

"No, it wasn't."

Bram runs his hand through his salt and pepper hair. "That's what I thought."

I expect him to ask more questions, but instead, he stays

quiet, like he's processing the little bit of information I just gave him.

Each passing minute is a vice being tightened on my heart. I flinch at every nurse or doctor that walks by, thinking it's going to be an update on Johnny.

A couple hours go by with no news. I hang tightly to the idea that he's still alive, because I cannot face a reality where he isn't.

"Do you want coffee?" Bram asks me. His features are riddled with nervous energy.

I nod, although there's nothing I truly want beyond Johnny.

In this same hospital is the man I visited earlier, the one that doesn't deserve the life left in him. Is this some kind of karmic balance for what I did to Griffin? Is what happened to Johnny somehow my fault because I was foolish enough to think I could poison Griffin and get away with it?

I'm not sure how long I'm lost in my own thoughts when Bram appears in front of me with a paper cup in his hand. "He's out of surgery."

I swear I feel my heart stutter in my chest. "What?"

"The doctor caught me on my way back. He's in recovery. The bullet missed all his major organs. Said Johnny must have had a guardian angel looking out for him. We can go back, but he's not awake yet. It could take a few hours before he's alert."

His words sink in one by one. The world seems to stop spinning. He's alive. Johnny is alive. By some fucking miracle, Franklin's plan failed.

Fresh tears roll down my cheeks. I rise to my feet and somehow, it's like a huge weight has been lifted off my shoulders. "Where is he?"

"This way." Bram leads me through a set of double doors and across a long hall. He pauses in front of a room and motions for me to enter.

I step inside, and all of my fears are quickly erased when my sights land on that beautiful, broken boy lying on the bed. The machines beep, telling me that he's very much still alive. That the world might not be as cruel as I had thought.

I silently thank the universe for sparing his life.

I'm at his side in an instant, gripping his hand in mine, but careful not to disturb him too much. A strong part of me wants to throw my arms around him and hold him tightly, kissing him all over and basking in the fact that he's here. I rein myself in, though, and settle for the comforting embrace of our fingers touching.

Bram pushes a chair forward for me. "Here."

I turn to him and swipe at the tears that won't seem to stop rolling down my cheeks. "He's alive."

Bram pulls me in for a hug.

I bury myself in his chest and put my arms around him.

"Everything is going to be okay," Bram reassures me.

And despite things being completely fucked up, knowing that Johnny made it through the impossible is enough to give me hope that Bram might be right.

"What do you need me to do? Can I get you guys a change of clothes?"

I wipe at my face and take a deep breath. I'm still covered in Johnny's blood and the debris from basically laying on the dirty street. I glance over to Johnny, sighing at just how young and vulnerable he appears. Rage tingles up my spine at the people responsible for putting him in this position. I shove it down—I can't focus on that right now. Not while things are in limbo.

Johnny may have escaped death tonight, but that doesn't mean he's in the clear just yet.

"Yeah, clothes would be good. I have an overnight bag already packed at Johnny's place. It's sitting on the couch in the living room. You'll have to grab his stuff, though. The gray sweatpants on the corner of his bed are his favorite. Maybe get his toothbrush, too. I'm sure he'll want to brush his teeth." I fumble in my pocket and pull out my keys. I slide the one

Johnny had given me off and hand it to Bram. "Oh, my access code, to the building—six two one three."

Bram nods his head with each one of my requests like he's taking an order at the diner. "Got it. Anything else?"

"No, that should be it." I glance over at Johnny and then back to Bram. "Thank you."

Bram leaves us behind, and I settle into the chair he had pulled up for me. I take Johnny's hand in mine and bring it to my lips. I press them gently along his skin and close my eyes, grateful for the warmth of life left in him.

I don't know what I would have done if I lost Johnny. A darkness creeps to the surface at the possibility. A version of me that would have stopped at nothing to make Franklin and his whole organization pay for what they had unfairly taken. It's still there, just simmering under the surface, partially at ease since Johnny really did make it through such a brutal attack.

I lay my head next to his thigh and hold his palm against my face, savoring the calmness his touch brings me. I imagine his fingers grazing my skin, his thumb doing that thing along my cheek that he always does.

Only, I'm not imagining it at all, it's real.

"Is that coffee I smell?" His voice is barely a whisper, cracking with each word spoken.

I can't help but break into a huge smile, tears streaming down despite having cried more than I thought humanly possible.

"Hey...it can't be that bad, right?" He grins and then winces, clutching his side in the process. "That feels terrible."

"Are you okay?"

Johnny reaches for me. "Come here."

I stand from the chair and approach him hesitantly. I don't want to cause him any more pain than he's already in.

He grabs my face with his hand, gripping it firmly while eyeing me over. "Are *you* okay?"

Leave it to Johnny to be concerned with someone else even though he's the one lying in the hospital bed, a true testament to how selfless he is.

"I am now." I smooth his hair off of his brow. "I thought I lost you."

He shakes his head. "Can't get rid of me that easily." Johnny pulls me toward him, gently kissing my lips.

I'll never quite get used to the feeling I get with him. It's a mixture of bliss and the best possible high. It's euphoric and unlike anything I've ever known.

"Is it any good?" He points to the paper cup I had forgotten all about.

I shrug. "Not sure." I grab onto it and take a sip. "It's pretty gross."

"Let me try." He takes it from me and brings it to his mouth. "Smells burnt."

The door to the room opens and a round-faced nurse holding a chart walks in. "You're awake, that's great." She looks at me. "Could we have a few moments alone?"

I don't mean to, but I squeeze Johnny's hand. The idea of not being with him is almost too much to handle. I just got him back, and now I have to leave again? What if something happens while I'm gone?

Johnny tightens his grip on me, too. "It'll be okay. I'm not going anywhere, unless it's to get a better cup of joe." He holds out the cup for me to take. "I promise."

Painfully, I walk away and out of the room, each step a twisted knife to my heart. I lean against the wall and lower myself to the ground, pulling my knees to my chest and holding them tightly. I refuse to cry anymore, even though the combination of everything going on is overwhelming. I have to be strong, if not for me, for Johnny.

There's the sound of footsteps, and when I glance up, Bram picks up his pace.

"Did something happen?" His eyes widen.

I rise to my feet. "No. Everything is okay. There's a nurse in there. She wanted privacy."

Relief washes over him. "Oh. Okay."

A second later, the same woman steps out. "You're good to go back in. I just gave him a dose of pain medicine, though, so he might not be awake too much longer." She points inside. "There are blankets in the cabinet, and you're more than welcome to use the facilities."

She must be referring to the fact that I'm covered in blood from head to toe.

"Thanks," I tell her.

Bram and I enter the room, each of us taking a side of the bed.

"You had us worried, kid," Bram tells Johnny.

"Sorry, old man." His voice is slurring.

"Everything go okay?" I nod toward the door where the nurse just exited.

Johnny nods. "Yeah, she wanted to make sure I was in a *safe environment*, since I got shot and all."

Bram sets a bag and a drink carrier on the table attached to Johnny's bed and hands me the overnight bag that I had asked for.

"Oh man, is that *real* coffee?" Johnny glances over at the paper cup on the other table. "That shit is gross."

I grin at him. "Told you."

"Yeah, it was pretty bad. Figured I wouldn't torture you any more than you already have been." Bram opens the bag. "Donuts, too. But I'm not sure if you're allowed to have either."

Johnny fumbles through his drugged-up state to snatch the sack and pull one out. "I almost died. I think they can make an exception." He pops the lid on one of the cups to let it cool.

With each thing he does, I feel the weight continue to be

lifted from my chest. The burden of thinking I had lost him nearly crushed me completely.

"Does anyone else know I made it?" Johnny asks us with a curious look on his face.

I tilt my head at him. "I've been here the whole time."

Bram adds, "I snuck in while everyone was busy. Didn't talk to anyone at the diner."

"What are the chances they actually think I'm dead?"

"Well, considering I was convinced until I heard the medic say your blood pressure was low, I'd assume they're pretty high." I hate recalling this entire nightmare.

"Why?" Bram meets Johnny's gaze.

With the most serious of expressions, Johnny blurts out, "We're going to fake my death."

"What can I do?" Bram stares at Johnny with the same intensity.

JOHNNY – 3

NOW

*I*t's difficult to pretend everything is fine when things could quite literally explode at any moment.

From the second this entire elaborate plan was put in motion, I've been looking over my shoulder nonstop.

I was a fool for thinking I could outrun him.

Franklin Sharp, the man with eyes everywhere.

How did I think a nobody like me could evade him?

"Here." Pax shoves a red cup toward me, and the golden liquid sloshes around.

I take it from him gratefully and down the contents in one motion. I wipe my lips and mutter, "Thanks."

Pax gawks at me with his beady eyes. He's been weird around me since the moment we met, but it's hard to blame him, considering he's known Claire for years and I'm a newcomer to the group.

She and I have been nothing but secrets and evasion, so it only makes sense to be skeptical of the random dude recovering from "appendicitis" surgery. I doubt the gunshot wound would have gone over very well, not to mention, it would have drawn too much unwanted attention to the truth of our double life.

How were we supposed to know that Pax's brother had the same surgery only a year ago? The recovery is fresh in his memory, alerting him to all the inconsistencies between the two.

Holland comes over and wraps her arm around Pax's shoulder. "How's my ginger friend doing?" Her words slur with the excess alcohol flooding through her. She blinks up at him and sways her body in a weak attempt to stand still.

He sighs and holds onto her in an attempt to keep her from falling down. "Hol. You're officially cut off." Pax carts her over to the couch and helps her sit. "You need water."

I turn my attention to the gorgeous girl across the room, the one with bright blue eyes and an ass to die for. I run my hand through my short hair, a habit I'm going to have to break. Another piece of the past I should put behind me.

I wink at Claire and she blushes in response, sending my heart galloping out of my chest.

Rosie rises from her seat and grabs the remote to the television, clicking the button to turn the volume up. "Thirty seconds!"

The small crowd gathers around. A few faces I'm familiar with; the rest are friends of Claire's friends I've met but forgotten their names.

Slowly, like it's only me and Claire left in the universe, I make my way over to her, our gazes glued to each other the entire way.

"Ten...nine..." The old man on the screen counts down.

My hand finds her cheek, resting gently along her flawless face. I breathe her in and savor just how lucky I am to have her here with me now. "I love you, Claire Cooper."

"Two...one..."

Claire smiles and pulls me toward her, pressing her soft lips against mine as people in the room erupt into cheers for the New Year.

Our mouths dance together in a heated frenzy that has me wishing we really were the only ones around. Over the past few months, the chemistry between us has managed to keep growing despite being at an all-time high. I didn't realize it was possible to be *this* damn attracted to someone. But I guess when you completely fall for someone, the way Claire and I have, it makes sense.

You would think the shit that we've been through would have torn us apart by now, but it's somehow made us stronger. There isn't a person I trust more in the world than the girl standing in front of me. And if I had to wager, I'd say she felt the same about me. That's why we work so well—we can count on one another. That's something neither one of us has really known before. Safety, security, the predictability of having someone in your corner looking out for you and actually giving a fuck.

It's refreshing to finally have someone truly care.

Claire breaks away and leans her forehead against mine. She keeps her voice low. "I love you, Johnny Jones."

"Happy New Year!" Rosie calls out while gripping me and Claire both by the shoulder. She's had her fair share of booze tonight, but it's safe to say she can handle her liquor much better than Holland can.

"Happy New Year," I tell her.

Rosie was always the wildcard with our situation. I knew the bond that she and Claire had runs deep, and there was no way she wouldn't be included in our future together. But managing what bits of information we gave her was like maneuvering through a minefield. Somehow, she did the impossible and surprised the hell out of me when she totally went along with the hidden identity thing. She didn't miss a beat in switching from calling me Johnny to Theo and, to this day, hasn't questioned us or slipped up on any of the details.

It's a lot to put on a person, especially without giving them the entire story.

But Claire and Rosie have something special. And because Rosie trusted Claire, and Claire trusted me, we built this circle of confidence in each other.

Plus, I really think it's helped Claire overcome the extremes of everything that has happened, by having her friend somewhat know what was going on. I can't imagine how rattled Claire must have felt, given the insane things that have happened in the last six months of her life.

Not only did she have to move across the country to live with her estranged mother, in a completely foreign place, but she had to sever ties with an abusive ex, nearly get killed, get wrapped up in the mess of my life, only to move *again* while trying to protect my identity from a sick and twisted criminal mastermind. Plus, all the details in between, like the shit with Jared, thinking I died, and balancing her school life.

Claire is a freaking saint.

She slips her hand into mine and holds on tight.

"So, Theo," Pax says.

I accidentally hesitate but end up looking at him. "Yeah?" I watch his freckled face and wait for whatever is about to come out of his mouth.

He's easily a few inches taller than me, but I could probably take him if I had to.

I hate that things have resorted to me sizing other people up, *just in case*. This world has taught me that you can never be too sure about who will or won't turn on you.

"You're not starting classes this week with the rest of us?" Pax pushes up the sleeves to his navy shirt, revealing ink on both arms.

"Nope."

"Why not?"

What's with the twenty questions?

Claire speaks up. "He's taking some time off."

Pax takes a swig of his beer. "I think the man can speak for himself, right?" He tips the cup up, drinking the rest and then crushing it in his hand. He tosses it into the trash can a few feet to his left.

Is that supposed to somehow intimidate me?

"I'm taking some time off," I repeat Claire's words.

She tightens her grip on me.

Pax points to my stomach. "To recover."

"Sure." If that's what he wants to tell himself, then so be it.

This dude has some keen intuition alerting him that *something* isn't quite accurate in my story. It's hard to be mad at him, but it could very well ruin everything if he uncovers the truth.

I can't start school with Claire because I haven't gotten my fake I.D. yet. And without it, I can't exactly register for classes. Going about normal daily activities under an alias is difficult enough, but bypassing college registration is a whole other hurdle.

I'd give anything to be there, to continue my education, and most of all, keep an eye on Claire, especially with the new information that's presented itself tonight. But I can't. Not yet. Not until I have more pieces put in place.

And not while I'm trying to figure out how in the hell I'm going to end this thing with Franklin once and for all. I should have known that faking my death would be step one, not the final move. If I'm going to do this, I have to see everything through and find a way to sever ties completely.

Now that Claire's location has been compromised, the matter becomes that much more pressing. I cannot allow him to use her as a pawn in his twisted game.

"I think it's great," Rosie chimes in. "I'm considering taking a semester off, too."

Her lie is so good it even fools Claire.

"What?" Claire's eyes go wide. "Bitch, you better not."

Rosie winks at me and then shrugs nonchalantly. "People do

it all the time."

Pax keeps his sights trained on me for an extra few seconds before taking the bait and diverting his attention to Rosie.

I'm really going to owe that girl one when this is all said and done.

"Me too," Holland mumbles from the couch. She throws her arm into the air and rolls onto the floor with a thud. "Ow."

Pax sighs and picks her up, throwing her over his shoulder. "This one has had enough. I'm going to take her home."

The way he easily tosses her around makes me second-guess whether or not I actually stand a chance against him. Maybe it's best if I don't find out. I either need to avoid him or get him on my good side if I'm going to keep my secrets hidden.

He says his goodbyes and carries Holland through the front door, disappearing into the night.

"Are those two a couple?" I ask Claire when I realize I've never actually seen them hold hands or kiss, but they're always together.

Claire and Rosie laugh at the same time.

"They've been best friends since kindergarten," Claire tells me.

Rosie adds, "Meaning, they're in love, they just don't know it yet. We know it. Everyone knows it. But for some fucking reason, they're still absolutely unaware."

I raise my head slowly. "Ohh. That explains it." I shift the focus of the conversation. "Thanks for the save."

Claire darts her attention to me and then Rosie.

"Hey, what are friends for?" Rosie takes a sip from her cup.

"Wait, you're not actually contemplating taking time off?"

Rosie rolls her eyes and grabs Claire's wrist. "And miss a moment with you? Are you crazy?"

And it may only be a tiny fraction of relief, but at least I know that even if I'm not there, Claire will have Rosie there looking out for her.

CLAIRE – 4

*J*ohnny has been acting strange. But I'm not sure if it's a normal strange, or a new strange.

Clearly, life has been a bit weird since the whole *faking his death* thing.

If I had to guess, he's feeling a bit off since I'm starting classes today and he won't be there. I can only imagine how difficult it is for him to not be able to watch over me. But we have to move on from the darkness of our past if we stand any chance of making it through this.

We've been in my hometown for nearly two months, and nothing has happened. No sign of Franklin or his goonies. No indication that he's aware of what we did to escape him. No threats or dangers looming around us. Just normal, everyday life. Well, as normal as we allow.

And part of our plan was for me to go back to school. Because that's the "reason" why I'm here on the East Coast, to return to the college I wanted to go to, with the scholarship I worked my ass off for. Only, the paperwork still hasn't arrived, and Johnny is actually covering my tuition this semester. Something I very much did not want to happen.

He insisted, though, and continues to reassure me that it's not a big deal for him to cover it. Between all of the expenses we've incurred during our escape, he has to be running low on funds, right? How is it possible he managed to save that much money while working for Franklin?

We've moved into three different apartments, and he even bought a used car. He put it in my name, since he can't exactly use his. Johnny hasn't blinked twice about the cash he's spending, and he doesn't seem to be stopping anytime soon. He isn't out buying pointless stuff, but even our necessities have to be adding up.

Johnny brings my hand to his lips and brushes my knuckles against them. "Let me know if you need me? I can be there in a second."

I can sense how nervous he is to let me go. At least one of the perks of our latest move is that it puts our new house within two blocks of the university. Johnny insists that I drive the little Volkswagen, but he'll be within walking distance if anything goes wrong. Another selling point of this unit is the gated entry and the fire escape access on the backside. It hasn't been easy to find what Johnny was looking for while making sure we could do month-to-month cash payments. Living under the radar poses its challenges, but he's done a damn good job making it all work.

"I will." I pull out my phone and show it to him. "Fully charged." I bring it toward me to let the facial recognition unlock the screen. I poke around until I find what I'm looking for. "And you have my location at all times." I zoom out and point to a few spots. "I'll be in this area the first few hours. Then this for the rest. I think the parking lot is here."

He sighs and bites at the inside of his lip.

I wish there was something more I could do to ease his nerves, like tucking him into my back pocket and letting him come with me for the day. I wouldn't mind it, really, having him around. But with things still so up in the air, we're trying to limit his public appearances. A little more time needs to pass and then *maybe* we'll feel safer.

For now, though, I need to keep up my own kind of appearances by being a normal person my age and following through with the plan of going to school.

I slide Johnny's fleece-lined denim jacket over my sweatshirt and toss my backpack over my shoulder. "You sure you're okay with me wearing this?"

His lip turns up in the corner. "Yeah. You look adorable." Johnny grabs my cheeks in his hands and kisses my mouth.

I'd be lying if I said I wasn't missing the heat of the sunny West Coast. I hadn't been there long, but damn if I didn't get used to that nonstop warmth, the ability to wear shorts and T-shirts, and the constantly beaming sun. In my time there, it had only rained once—the day of Johnny's fake funeral. It was fitting, really, totally setting the mood for our master plan. But other than that, it was bright and sunny and nothing like this winter doom and gloom it's been replaced by.

Don't get me wrong, the first day it snowed here, it was glorious. The look on Johnny's face was priceless. But once the new wore off, and the messy slush replaced the bright white wonderland, I started crossing my fingers that the stupid groundhog won't see his shadow next month. A girl can still hope for an early spring.

I drive the short distance to school, making sure to avoid all of the new potholes created by the snowplows. I pull into my designated spot and put the car into park. Because I'm sure he's already stressed out, I send Johnny a quick text.

Me: I made it. Miss you already xo
Johnny: Miss you more. Be safe walking to class.

I swipe over to Rosie.

Me: You here yet?

Rosie: I see you!!!

I turn and look all around me until I spot her coming toward me. She's wearing a dark green sweatshirt and her golden blonde hair is in a neat ponytail, bobbing with each step she takes. There's a huge smile across her face, and it makes me feel a little less alone without having Johnny here with me.

"I'm so excited," she squeals when she opens my door.

I jump out and grab my bag, clicking the button on the key fob to lock the car. "Just like it was always supposed to be." I weave my arm through hers, and we take off toward the main building.

So much has changed since Rosie and I originally planned to go here. Six months ago, I was dating Griffin, held under his thumb and living a completely different version of my life, one that seems completely foreign when I reflect on it. Now, I'm stronger, broken down but somehow built up to a newer, better Claire. One that I don't think would have been possible without Johnny. He gave me the strength to find my inner power and overcome the shit life decided to throw my way. He helped shape me into the woman I am today.

Johnny gives me something I've never had before—a choice. A voice. The freedom to be me without judgment and concern that I won't be accepted.

All Griffin wanted to do was bring me down.

It's been weeks since I did what had to be done, and I'm still not sure what the outcome was. It's not exactly like I can call and ask if he's alive. I have to wait it out and see what happens. And then hope like hell I don't get caught.

There's a very real chance that poisoning Griffin did not work, but there's still a chance it did. Either way, I will keep that secret with me to the grave. Johnny has loved me through so much, but could he handle knowing I killed someone, and that I did it intentionally?

That might be too much for anyone to bear.

I wouldn't blame him for seeing me as a monster, but I'm not sure that's a reality I'm willing to face. What if I lose him? When I followed through with poisoning Griffin, I was trying to put him in the past. I wanted to sever ties with him and stop allowing him from controlling my life. But little did I know, there's no escaping someone who has their claws *that* deeply sunk into you.

"I've heard this creative writing class is the *bomb*." Rosie puts a little extra flair on that last word. "Hey." She glances over at me. "You okay?"

I nod and lie. "Yeah." I didn't realize being away from Johnny would be this...uncomfortable. We've been together nonstop for the past few months, aside from errands here and there, so spending *hours* away at school day after day will be the longest we've been apart. Maybe if we hadn't been through such traumatic shit, I wouldn't feel this way, but we have, and pretending to be a normal college kid is weirder than I thought it was going to be.

"Ah, you and JJ." She glances around. "Sorry, *Theo*." Rosie grips me tighter. "Makes sense. But listen, I'll be with you, so you aren't alone."

What if it's not me I'm worried about? What if it's Johnny? I have Rosie, and I get to at least play the part of a functioning person in society. Johnny is stuck all cooped up in our apartment worried sick that something will happen to me, or someone will come for him. There has to be *some* way to give him his life back so he's not constantly afraid of endless possibilities.

We walk into the classroom and go toward the back. I haven't been in such a crowded space since everything went down, so choosing a seat where I can keep my eyes on everyone puts me a little at ease. From here, I have a clear view of the door, too. Although, given there is only one exit, I'll have to get creative if something were to happen.

Is that what life is going to be like now? Constantly looking for a way out? Thinking everyone around me is a potential suspect? Until Franklin, I was naive to the world around me. I thought the shit that I witnessed first-hand was only stuff they made up in the movies. Witnessing Jared and Steve bleed out in that alley by Bram's, and Johnny getting shot not too long after, made me realize just how cruel people really can be.

Everything that Jared had done to me aside, did he and Steve really deserve to be shot and left for dead? They were someone's children, friends, maybe significant other. With all the time I've spent with Johnny, I know damn well that he never deserved the endless beatings and the near-death experience. Who gave Franklin the right to play God? To end someone's life because they inconvenienced him?

I guess at the end of the day, I'm not much better than him, considering what I did to Griffin.

But if anyone should be cowering in hiding, it should be me, not Johnny. He's given up so much and for what? To live in constant fear? How is that fair?

"You okay?" Rosie asks me.

I snap out of my trance and bob my head up and down. "Yeah, sorry, zoned out." I unzip my bag and pull a notebook out. If I'm going to be here, I might as well pay attention. I won't allow Johnny's hard-earned blood money to go to waste.

"Welcome," the curly-headed, middle-aged man at the front of the room says. "I'm Professor Adkins. If you're here with us now, please note that you are in Advanced Creative Writing. Course number three-oh-one."

A few students fumble with their bags and exit through that one door.

Our teacher lets out a chuckle. "Happens every time." He leans against his desk and scans the rest of us.

Rosie kicks my foot from under the table, drawing my attention. She raises her brows and cocks her head over at the professor.

"No," I mouth and shake my head.

She juts out her bottom lip. "Why not?"

"One," I whisper. "That's totally unprofessional, two, he's *old.*"

Rosie sighs. "Fine."

"You can grab your kits on the way out when class is dismissed." Professor Adkins crosses his arms. "Anyone have any questions about that?"

Shit. I have no idea what he said. Kits for what? This isn't exactly the best way to start my first class. Maybe taking some of my classes with Rosie was a bad idea after all. It's fun, that's for sure, but it's hella distracting, too.

"Great." He grabs a stack of papers from his desk and distributes them to the front of the class, mumbling something to the students and getting them to pass the pages back. "As you'll see, the ancestry results will be interpreted into your final paper, along with coinciding with most of your assignments throughout the course."

Ancestry? Is that what he meant when he was referring to the kits? That would make sense. What a strange thing to do in a creative writing class, though.

"I find that sometimes the best work comes from within, from our own experiences and those of our past. If we tap into that, and follow along with the prompts provided, I think there will be great results."

What, was he reading my mind or something?

"I'm sure you have your doubts, but trust me with this. Most people are completely unaware of their heritage." He goes back to leaning against his desk. "Now, on the other hand, if you already have an established knowledge, feel free to skip the test. You'll still be required to do the work, but if you're aware of yours, there's no need to do the analysis. We will be going back five generations, so if you have that covered, you're good to go."

What do I know about my lineage? Not much. Aside from my dad's mom, who died when I was little, it's always just been me and Dad. I never really asked about my own mother's family, since she was such an absent part of my life. I guess I assumed if there was anyone else, they would have cared enough to come forward.

My thoughts linger on Johnny and what little he's told me about his family. His mother died when he was young, and he never knew his dad. He has a cousin who's in the military, but I'm not sure if they were even blood-related.

There's Bram, but he was just a part of Johnny's found family, a father-figure role that Johnny never had. A piece of the past that I'm certain Johnny never wanted to give up.

I can't fix everything that's happening right now, with Franklin, but what if there was a way I could bring Johnny some insight into who his family might actually be? Maybe that would bring him the littlest bit of peace in this chaotic time in his life. I owe him at least that.

JOHNNY – 5

ALMOST TWO MONTHS AGO

I hate how fucking weak I am.

There's too much that needs to be done, and I'm in no shape to do it all myself.

The perfect opportunity has presented itself, and I have to take advantage of it.

Franklin may have thought he had the upper hand, but he underestimated my ability to adapt to whatever is thrown my way.

I never meant to involve anyone else in this twisted world of mine, but if I'm going to make it out of this, I'm going to have to get some outside help.

Starting with Claire and Bram.

The machines I'm attached to beep in the background. I keep my voice low but loud enough for them to hear. "I'll need a new burner phone and the contact to get in touch with someone at the coroner's office." I hold onto Claire's hand and brace myself for what I'm about to ask of her. "Claire, you're in charge of planning my funeral."

Her eyes go wide, but she doesn't say anything. I can sense

her unease but if this plan is going to work, we have to go through the motions as if it really happened.

"Do either of you trust any cops that are willing to take a bribe?"

Bram speaks up from his spot at the foot of my hospital bed. "I have a guy in mind."

"Good. But you need to be sure, okay? We can't make any mistakes with this."

"Got it." Bram stands from his chair. "I'm on it." He looks at Claire. "Call me if you need anything else in the meantime."

Bram goes, making sure to latch the door shut behind him.

"You okay?" I rub Claire's hand with my thumb.

"How are we going to pull this off?" Her blue eyes stare into me.

"Do you trust me?"

She blinks up at me. "Of course, I do."

"You're distraught, Claire. Your boyfriend just died. It makes total sense for you to leave this place behind and go home. You got a scholarship to pay for school, and have enough money saved to get your own apartment." I go over the story she's going to tell anyone from back home if it's brought up.

Rosie is the only one who knows about me, so she's the only one who needs to know anything. Everyone else? Claire followed through with her plan to win that scholarship and is returning home the way she always intended.

"But I don't have that kind of cash. And I have no clue when the award will be processed." Claire second-guesses my cover story.

"That part isn't important; I have it covered."

Claire narrows her eyes. "That's too much. And with everything else? There's no way."

"I'm telling you. The financial aspect of this entire thing is the last thing you should be concerned with." I don't know how else to make her realize her worries are misplaced without actually showing her how much money I have saved.

"What about that?" She points toward the bandage wrapped around my torso.

"I'll figure that out, too. We'll make stops along the way. Speaking of, I'll have to figure out a car, preferably with deeply tinted windows."

An idea seems to spark in Claire's mind. "Beth's BMW. It's the least she could do for being such a shit mom, and it totally fits in with the story we're telling." Claire's brief optimism is quickly erased. "Shit, what am I going to tell my dad?"

I soften my voice. "Have you talked to him?"

"No. But I'm going to have to. I can't just move back across the country and not let him know." Claire picks at her thumb. "What am I going to say to Rosie?"

I reach down and tilt her chin up. "We're going to figure this out, all of it." It suddenly dawns on me that I never gave Claire a choice in any of this. What if this isn't what she wants? To be with me? To risk everything and help me with this elaborate plan to evade a man that tried to kill me.

I'd do all of this again if it meant setting Billy free from the claws Franklin was trying to sink into him. But just because I'm willing to take insane chances doesn't mean Claire is, and I shouldn't assume this is what she wants.

"What's wrong?" Claire grips my hand tighter.

It's like she can see straight through me and into my soul.

One thing I always promised myself was that I would put Claire first, and the only way I can do that is by allowing her to make her own decision in this matter, even if it fucking kills me. "You're allowed to walk away."

She squints her brows. "What?"

"If this is too much. I'd understand if you didn't want to be a part of it anymore."

Claire pulls her hand away. "Are you trying to break up with me?"

"No." I reach for her but stop myself. "I'm just making sure you know you have a choice. That you're not forced to be here. And I wouldn't be mad at you if you've changed your mind. About any of this."

It rips my heart apart to open that theoretical door, but it would hurt me, even more, to not give her the option. I will never force myself or this fucked-up situation on her. After everything she's been through, she deserves much better, and I refuse to disallow that from happening. If Claire is going to stay, it's going to be *her* decision, not anyone else's.

"Do you want me here?" There's a slight hesitation behind her voice, like she might actually believe otherwise.

"You know I do, but I need *you* to be sure. This isn't up to me." Because at the end of the day, I care more about Claire than I do myself.

Claire weaves her fingers around mine and stares at me intensely. "I'm not going anywhere, not without you."

I should stop her. I should say no. I should tell her the risks over and over again until she realizes how insane all of this is. I should convince her that she isn't safe and that she should run far away from me. But I can't. I'm too weak to let her go. I've never needed anything like I need Claire.

I clear my throat. "Then it's settled, we do this. And we do it together."

There's so much left to plan. Like how to get out of the hospital without anyone noticing. Arranging medical care on our trip across the country. Getting everyone that will be involved on board with lying about my death and pulling off a believable funeral. I'll have to get my stuff from my place, plus all the cash stashed all over my house. I'll need a fake I.D. and a new alias to go by. Luckily, people are highly motivated by money, and with the excess I have, making this plan work might actually be possible.

I'll have to find me and Claire a place to live, and secure us some kind of permanent transportation once we're done with Beth's car. Most of all, I have to do everything in my power to stay alive and keep Claire safe.

I've never traveled outside of my home state, but what better time to start than now? It's completely irrational, but it's the only thing I can think of to slip from Franklin's grasp. He's made it clear that he will stop at nothing to make sure I'm finished. Maybe if he truly believes I'm dead, he'll forget I ever existed and move on with his fucked-up life.

I will jump from this ledge, Claire's hand in mine, ready to dive headfirst into what I hope to be a fresh new beginning.

CLAIRE – 6

NOW

How am I going to get Johnny's saliva on this test tube without telling him what it is?

It's not that I want any more secrets between us, but he's dealing with enough on his own, I'd rather present him with *good* news, not news that will make him nervous while we wait for the results.

What if his family is full of a bunch of serial killers? Or they're all dead? What if there is no one left and it really is just Johnny? I'd rather carry that burden for him until he's ready for it. But, what if he has living grandparents that own a bakery and go to bingo every Thursday and had no idea they had a grandson? There's a possibility that Johnny might have someone *other* than me and Bram, and I'd love to be able to give him that.

"You okay?" Johnny asks from his spot at our dining room table. He wipes his mouth on a napkin and takes a drink of his tea.

"Yeah." I change the subject. "How was your day?"

His jaw twitches, showing the slightest hint of tension, a cue that a random person would never notice. But I'm tuned-in enough to Johnny to recognize when something is bothering him. "It was all right."

I pop a French fry into my mouth. "Mmhm."

I guess we're both holding back from each other.

"I worried about you all day," he admits, although I'm not so sure that's the thing nagging at him.

I reach across the table and squeeze his hand. "But we did it. First day of school. No issues. Nothing major happened."

He glances over at me with the last part. "But something minor?"

I smile and shake my head. "No. It went smoothly, really."

"And the roads weren't bad?"

"Nope. Not with snow. There's a huge fucking pothole near the parking lot entrance, but other than that, it was fine." *Oh, and I want a sample of your DNA to see if you have any living relatives.* I keep that bit to myself though.

I could easily just ask him. Johnny would probably do anything for me. But there's the chance he says no. That he's fine not knowing about his family because he's okay with where he is—with me. That can't be it, though; if there are others out there, shouldn't he at least *know* about them? Then he can make the choice as to whether or not he wants anything to do with them. That's what I would want. But I shouldn't assume he has the same mindset. And that's why I'd rather figure it out first and *then* tell him if there's something that needs to be told. It would be unfair of me to unravel any unwanted emotions without having any details to follow them up with.

Johnny grazes my arm with his finger. "What's up with you?"

I glance over to meet his concerned look. This is where I open up my mouth and ask him the nagging question I can't get out of my head. When I learn the truth of how he really feels about the mystery behind his past.

Instead, I say, "Do you have any food allergies?"

His luscious brows bunch together. "What?"

I urge my raging heart to slow its pace. "Yeah, like dairy or gluten? Peanuts maybe?"

Johnny scratches his temple. "I'm not following."

I bite at the inside of my lip, forcing myself to come up with the rest of my lie. "In my nutrition class, we're doing this test to see if we have any. I was just wondering if you did."

It's not completely farfetched. I am taking a nutrition course. And we did discuss this very topic. But we're not actually checking for them, at least not that I'm aware of.

"Oh." Johnny blinks. "No. I don't think so." He pauses then adds, "Do you?"

I shake my head. "Me either. But I have an extra swab if you wanted to make sure." I let out a breath. "Hate to go through everything you have and then end up killing over from a random shellfish allergy."

Johnny hesitantly buys my story. "Yeah, sure. I'll take it with you. What do you need from me? Blood or something?"

I refrain from showing the emotion that's nearly seeping from my pores as I make my way over to my backpack and pull out the little vial. "Just a cheek swab." I hold it out and smile at him. I recall the details the professor had given us about making sure we hadn't eaten or drank anything within thirty minutes of taking the test. "But we'll have to wait."

Johnny holds out his arms to me, a seductive grin on his beautiful face. The faint outlines of scars linger on his skin. One near his brow, another on his cheek, the bottom of his lip. Memories from a time I hope he never has to visit again. "I can think of something we can do to pass the time."

I walk over to him, fitting myself between his legs while he sits on the barstool. "Yeah? What's that?"

"I was hoping you'd ask." His green eyes melt into me, trailing their way over my skin. He leans forward and brings his mouth to my ear, his breath warm on my neck. "Claire." His whisper sends a decadent chill along my eager body. Johnny runs his nose across my skin, leaving a wake of soft kisses on his journey to my mouth. He pauses, his lips lingering barely on mine.

My heart pounds heavily, but instead of it being because of my secret, it's for him, and him alone. The desire I have for him has never diminished in the slightest, and if anything, I want him more with each passing day. The more we explore each other, both sexually and emotionally, the stronger our bond becomes.

Some people go their whole lives not having the chance to experience what we share. It's solid and fierce and passionate. Raw and real, and unlike anything I ever could have imagined.

Every touch is a beautiful fire rippling across my skin. Every look is enough to send a hidden message from one to the other. There's trust and devotion, loyalty, and selflessness. There's something magical that I would go to the ends of the earth to fight for, to make sure I could hold onto it as long as humanly possible.

The best part of all—it's mutual.

As absolutely crazy as I am for Johnny, I feel it reciprocated wholly. And maybe that's what stokes our flame higher, the constant flow of love we pour into our relationship. It's cliché as fuck to say, but we really are each other's ride or die.

I would do anything for Johnny. And I know he would do the same.

Johnny brings his lips to mine, caressing them softly. They're a perfect fit, like two puzzle pieces locking into place. Our mouths, our bodies, our hands, even our personalities, and the things we have in common…two beings that were made to complete the other. Where I end, he begins, making each other whole.

He's in tune with my every breath and knows what I want before I do.

I bring my hands instinctually to his head, to tangle them in his hair. I smile into him when the short bristle of his new cut tickles my palms.

Johnny stands, causing me to take a step back. He grips my waist and guides me to the couch.

I clutch the hem of his T-shirt and drag it up and off of him. My fingers run down the front of his chest, pausing on his stomach. I sigh, taking my attention and shifting it toward his injury. "Are you in any pain?"

Johnny moves to unbutton my pants. "The only thing causing me discomfort right now is all this damn space between us." His intense stare bores into me.

We've been taking things slow since his accident, trying to be extra cautious considering we didn't want to have any unexpected complications with his recovery. It's one thing to find a shady doctor that won't ask too many questions to assess his healing, but it's another if he's rushed to the emergency room if something was to go wrong. He's pretty much made it out of the thick of it, but I still worry that our *extra-curriculars* could pose a risk, especially when he was obviously straining the first time we messed around after getting here.

"Claire, I promise. No pain. I'm good. More than good." He tips my chin up with his finger. "I want to feel you."

His words are my undoing.

I drop down onto the couch, grabbing his jeans and boxers in one motion, and yank them over his hips.

Johnny's hands tangle in my hair as I grip the base of him and swirl my tongue around his tip. A moan escapes his lips, and I continue to tease. I barely get a taste before he's pulling away.

"Turn over." He points to the couch.

Something about his demanding tone has me complying without another thought.

I climb up, my back to him as my knees rest on the cushion.

I glance over my shoulder at him, waiting for him to make his move.

Johnny weaves his fingers under the seam of my panties and slides them over my ass, exposing me to him. He lowers himself to the edge of the couch, bringing his face closer and closer until he's hovering his mouth along my slit.

I lean over the couch and arch my back, spreading my legs to give him better access.

He obliges by grabbing my hips and burying his face deeper, his tongue gliding up and down, his lips feverishly dancing all over me. If I was wet earlier, I'm soaked now—my desire to feel him inside me growing with each passing second of his playful exploration.

Johnny slides a digit into me, the thickness telling me it's his thumb. He rubs it in circles while he continues to lick in all the right places.

"Johnny," I breathe. I don't know how much of this I can handle. I need to feel *him*.

As if he reads my mind, he does one final pass with his tongue, nearly sending me over the edge. He leaves his thumb in place, gently rocking it back and forth while he fumbles to grab a condom.

I reach back, gripping and stroking him, trying to guide him closer to my entrance.

After what seems like forever, he bites off the corner of the condom wrapper and with one hand slides the sheath over his shaft.

I inch back, dropping my knees even further apart.

He glides his thumb out and up as he positions himself in place. His movements are slow and purposeful, where mine are rushed and greedy. This perfect dynamic of push and pull drives me completely fucking wild.

I rock back, allowing the length of him to enter me.

"Fuck," he moans.

I push against him, matching his rhythm and noting the steady build of his breaths.

His pleasure only continues to heighten mine.

For this temporary moment, there is nothing in the world except me and him, our bodies joined together in a beautiful chaos.

Johnny leans down while reaching for me, bringing his head closer to mine to tilt it to him and find my lips. He continues thrusting, a slow and steady, deep tempo.

The seconds our mouths collide, we hungrily kiss each other, rocking our bodies together more and more and more until our orgasm rattles through us at the exact same time, as though we're completely in sync with one another.

Johnny's breath fans over me as he rests his forehead against mine, his throbs inside of me send a vibration through my body that morphs into a shiver of pure pleasure. He kisses my shoulder softly, leaving a sweet trail on his way back up, then slides out of me carefully so we can both collapse into the couch.

I study the rise and fall of his chest, my eyes gazing down at the puckered wound from the gunshot that almost took him from me.

I'm forever thankful for whatever saving grace kept him in my life that day. But no matter how much I try to convince myself to leave the past in the past, I'm not sure I can. One way or another, I will find a way to make Franklin pay for what he's done. For torturing the man I love and putting him through things no one should have to go through. It might take me the rest of my life to figure it out, but Franklin will get what's coming to him if it's the last thing I do.

Johnny wipes at his forehead with his shoulder. He glances over at me. "Want to shower?"

JOHNNY - 7

I keep waiting for something else to happen, but nothing does.

Part of Franklin's game is psychological warfare, and he does a damn good job at it. That one little sheet of paper slipped into our mail was enough to completely unhinge me. It was clever, if you think about it: a self-inflicted torture while he stays in the shadows, watching from the sidelines, waiting to attack.

If only I could find a way to end this once and for all; then I could go back to living my life, resume some kind of normalcy with the woman I love. Maybe we could go out on real dates and do things with her friends and not have to worry about someone posting us on social media. I could go back to school and focus on doing shit people my age do.

And maybe I could visit Bram without having to risk getting killed.

Leaving my old life behind wasn't too difficult, considering I had already given up so much in my attempt to save Billy from Franklin, but I hated having to say goodbye to the one person who stuck by me even when I went through some of my darkest days.

I wouldn't have made it this far without Bram. I'll never be able to repay him the kindness he showed me almost each and every day, and especially at the end, when he helped me and Claire orchestrate my escape. He did so without question, proving to me how much he really does care about me.

Claire's phone vibrates on the table, and after a quick glance at it, she pushes the button to silence it. She goes back to her studies without saying a word.

My old self would have ignored the weirdness of the situation and completely disregarded what just happened. But with things the way they are now, the unknown of who that could have been burns a hole straight through me. I open my mouth to speak, but I stop myself. If she wanted to tell me, she would. So why didn't she?

I'm not a jealous guy, but when Claire's life is in danger, I kind of need to know what the fuck is going on. It's a constant struggle to balance giving her the privacy she deserves while still keeping her safe.

I stare at the phone, wishing like hell I could set it on fire with my penetrating gaze so there was no way anyone could get in touch with her. At least, not until I figure out how to get Franklin out of our lives for good.

The thing buzzes again, alerting her to a voicemail.

I watch her intently and wait for some kind of reaction.

Finally, she sighs and swipes her screen to unlock it. Claire pokes at a few things until the crackle of the speaker comes to life.

Thank God, she put it on speakerphone. Now I won't have to be a completely overbearing boyfriend and ask her who it was.

A thick and familiar voice comes through. "Ms. Cooper, this is Officer Donovan."

Claire glances over at me and then back at her phone.

The officer continues, "If you could give me a call back at

your earliest convenience, it would be appreciated. You can reach me at my direct office line, or my cell. Thanks."

The line shuts off and a mixture of relief and confusion settles through me.

It wasn't Franklin. It wasn't another weird message that could be interpreted as a threat. Since we relocated to this new, more private building, there hasn't been a single thing out of place to cause alarm. Although, it's only a matter of time until he finds us again. Hence why I'm jumpy at every damn thing.

But a call from Officer Donovan isn't great either, because that means it has something to do with Griffin, Claire's no-good, abusive, piece of shit ex who tried to ruin her life and even attempted to throw her down a flight of stairs. The one who I ended up sending down the stairs instead and into a critical condition that might cost him his life.

If he's calling, does that mean Griffin woke up? Did he come to and tell the officer the truth about the situation? That I was the reason for his condition? That I assaulted him and that he's pressing charges? What if he has some kind of proof, or someone that's a witness to what went down that night?

Franklin isn't the only person who could potentially ruin my life. Griffin could, too.

And that sends another shockwave of fear rushing through me.

Who will protect Claire if I'm put behind bars? Franklin would sure enough finish me off if I got locked up. He has connections everywhere—a simple handshake full of cash would end my life quicker than a snap of the fingers.

Claire stares at her phone, not breaking her gaze until I walk over and sit across from her.

I place my hand on top of hers, reassuring her that I'm here, despite the unstable uncertainties rushing through me.

She flinches at my touch—a painful reminder of the fear Griffin must have put in her throughout their time together.

I never want her to be afraid of me. I'm the last person on the planet who would ever hurt a hair on her beautiful head.

"Hey," I say gently. "Everything's going to be okay." I'm not sure if I'm reassuring her or myself. Although, it's safe to say we both need it.

"What if it's not?" There's more than fear in her eyes, but I can't quite place it.

I tilt my head slightly and sigh. "Claire. We're in this together, okay? No matter what happens."

She must be just as afraid as I am that Griffin came to and told his side of the story. Claire thought she lost me once; what if she loses me again? I don't think either one of us could handle that reality.

Claire bites her lip. "Promise?"

I give her a gentle squeeze. "Always." There isn't a damn thing in the world I wouldn't do for her. We've made it through some insane shit, and there's no stopping me from fighting for us until my very last breath.

She exhales and forces a weak smile. "Okay." Claire pushes the contact for Officer Donovan and clicks on the call button.

A second later, it begins ringing through the speakerphone again.

"This is Officer Donovan."

Her voice cracks, "Hi, this is Claire...Claire Cooper."

"Miss Cooper, good afternoon."

I swallow down the fear that rises up my throat.

Claire stares at the screen. "What can I help you with?"

Donovan continues, "There's no great way to put this, but I wanted to call and inform you; Griffin Thomas is dead."

I do my best to hide my shock. *He's dead?*

"Oh wow, really? What happened?" Claire shifts slightly in her seat.

"There were some complications. It's not at all uncommon

in situations like this. There will be an autopsy performed, but the final report will take some time to come in."

I let out a breath. *Complications.*

Claire tenses beside me.

"This isn't exactly the outcome we had hoped for. I was really optimistic our case was solid enough to put Mr. Thomas behind bars." He sighs. "But you can rest assured that he'll never be able to hurt anyone else ever again."

"Yeah." Claire's voice is barely a whisper.

"Anyway, I thought you'd like to know. If anything, for a little bit of peace of mind."

"Thank you for calling me."

"Of course. I truly am sorry, for what happened to you and to his other victims."

Chatter comes through the background of his call.

Donovan covers the receiver and says, "Just a minute." He brings his attention back to the call. "If you need anything, don't hesitate to reach out."

"Will do," Claire tells him.

The line disconnects and we're left sitting there in the silence. A short moment passes, and I grip Claire's hand, staring intently at her profile.

She stays still while her eyes dart from left to right like she's lost in thought.

I swallow. "Are you okay?"

What a loaded question to ask someone in a situation like this. Of course she's not. Her ex-boyfriend is dead. And although he was a monster who treated her poorly, he was still a person. What's worse? He's no longer alive because of me.

I killed him.

What if the shock rattling her features is caused by the realization that the man she's with *now* is a monster, too? What if, in defending Claire, I turned into something she could never look past?

All I've wanted to do was protect her, not make her fear me.

Claire lets out a long breath. "Yeah. I'm fine." She forces a smile and finally meets my gaze. "You want some coffee?"

Is she really in that big of a rush to get away from me? How long until she's gone for good? What if she can't get over what I've done?

My heart constricts, like a giant hand is gripping it tightly, threatening to never let go.

"Claire." Her name is soft and delicate on my lips. A gentle pleading with her to understand I'd never hurt her. To know that she's the only thing that truly matters in this world.

"Yeah?" She bites at her lip, concealing whatever emotions that are bubbling to the surface.

"Can we talk about this?" I've always given Claire a choice, but damn if I don't want to drop down on my knees and beg her to forgive me, to stay with me.

"What is there to talk about? He's dead, that's all that matters." Claire's jaw tenses.

I'd give anything to read her mind, to truly hear what it is that she's thinking right now. I scan her face, desperately trying to uncover any hidden cue to help me figure her out. I always do my best to be in tune with Claire, her wants and needs, but at this very moment, it's as though she has a wall up against me, not allowing me in. She's blocking me out, and that only tightens the fist around my heart even more.

"I'm..." I start to apologize, but I don't want to lie to her—I can't. I'm not sorry for what I did. And if killing Griffin was the only way to save her, I'd do it over and over again. Deep down, I think Claire realizes this, too. There isn't anything I wouldn't do to keep her from harm's way. I'd go to the ends of the earth and stop at nothing to make sure she was safe.

I guess that's what happens when you fall for someone the way I have for Claire.

Deeply, powerfully, and without any fucking reservations.

I may have pushed her away, but I don't regret doing what I know with certainty was the right thing to do. Griffin would have killed her himself if I didn't step in and stop him. If I have to lose Claire, I'd rather it be like this than at the hands of Griffin or some other sick fuck.

"You're what?" Claire waits for me to continue.

I say the only thing I can. "I love you."

I don't miss the way her shoulders relax in the slightest, the release of tension that flutters out of her. She reaches out and runs her finger along my cheek. "I love you."

And maybe, just maybe, I haven't lost her after all.

CLAIRE – 8

ALMOST TWO MONTHS AGO

In a dimly lit room a few blocks from our apartment, Johnny and Bram face each other for what will be the last time.

For now, maybe forever.

I try to give them the distance to say their goodbye, but with the confined space and the pull to my heartstrings, it's difficult not to pay attention to such a beautifully tragic moment.

The two embrace but are careful not to be too rough with Johnny's injury.

Under his shirt is a bandage-wrapped torso that will have to be checked periodically to make sure it's healing and not getting infected—something that should be done in the hospital, or at the least in a proper doctor's office.

We don't have that luxury anymore, not if we want Johnny to live through this.

If Franklin catches wind that Johnny is still alive, he'll be furious, and there's no telling how many casualties will pile up on his way to end Johnny once and for all.

Pulling this off will be no easy feat, but there isn't anything I wouldn't do to keep this man alive.

Volunteering to drive us across the country to flee a psychopath is nothing compared to the idea of going through life without Johnny. I witnessed the light drain from his eyes, and I thought I had lost him. My heart shattered, and I begged the universe to bring him back to me. Maybe I used up my one allotted miracle, maybe it was some kind of divine intervention, but whatever it was—I refuse to lose him again.

"When will I be hearing from you?" Bram keeps his hands planted firmly on Johnny's shoulders, looking him in the eyes.

I can feel the sadness radiating off the two of them. Neither one of them are good at this kind of thing, but in reality, who would be?

"I don't know," Johnny says, his voice a bit tattered. He's hurting, probably in more pain than he lets on, both physically and emotionally, but he's well aware of what needs to be done.

Bram sighs, releasing Johnny. He shakes his head. "I can't believe this is it."

The scene resembles something of a teenager going off to college, only more heartbreaking and permanent.

Johnny clears his throat, wincing in the process and sitting down to catch his breath. "Thank you, for everything."

Bram stands there like there are a million things unsaid between them. Yet all he replies with is, "Of course."

Johnny may have his secrets from Bram, but he's still there for him no matter what. Bram knows with certainty that Johnny is a good person, and that whatever he was involved with was for good reason. He blindly trusts and supports him at the distance Johnny keeps. That's why the second Johnny asked for his help, he leaped at the opportunity without asking any questions.

I may have only been around a few months, but the relationship between Johnny and Bram runs deep, something that exceeds bloodlines and time. They are family despite the lack of DNA linking them together, something I'm not sure either one of them realized they had until now, when they had to walk away from it.

"Do you have everything you need?" Bram glances between us.

I approach him, reaching my arm around his torso. "Yeah. Thanks."

Bram pulls me in for a hug and grips me tightly. "You take care of each other, okay?"

I don't miss the way he fights through the words in his attempt not to cry. Johnny is like a son to him, and I can't imagine the way this must break his heart to let him go this way.

It would be one thing if there was a plan in place, a possibility of being in each other's lives again, but with the magnitude of the situation, this could be it. It would be unfair to give anyone unrealistic expectations of a future so unknown.

I'd like to think we'll slip completely from Franklin's grasp, but that's a reality that might not be possible.

As much as I harbor a boundless well of hatred for Franklin, actually getting the revenge I want will be an incredibly challenging task. Especially if I want to keep Johnny safe. And at the end of the day, keeping him far from death's door is my greatest priority.

Johnny brings himself to his feet once more, a massive task considering the freshness of his injury. It's a wonder at all that he's able to do what he has in such a short time, let alone while healing from his surgery after he was shot.

One thing is certain, Johnny is a fighter, and no matter how far he's backed against a wall, he will do everything in his power to overcome the situation. It's how he's managed to exist in Franklin's world this long.

I give Bram a final squeeze and let him go.

He turns to Johnny. "You'll call me if you need me?"

Johnny nods and steps toward Bram.

But Johnny is lying. He's already put Bram in too much danger involving him at all, and he won't continue to risk his safety any more.

Bram envelopes Johnny into his arms, his eyes glistening with all the things he wants to say. "I'll be seeing you."

Johnny palms Bram's back, struggling to maintain his own emotions. "Yeah."

Their moment is brief, but powerful.

My heart constricts at the enormous love these two have for each other.

All three of us walk to the door, Johnny leading up the rear at a little slower pace. How he's up walking around, I'll never know. It's probably all adrenaline and fear.

Bram plants his hand on Johnny's shoulder one last time. He looks to me, then to Johnny, and takes his leave.

We stand there in the doorway, Johnny hidden from sight behind me, watching Bram walk away. He never turns around; he doesn't glance over his shoulder one last time. He just keeps going, one step after another, until there's no more of him, until he's gone.

"I have to do this," Johnny says through gritted teeth.

"I don't doubt you."

"This is the only way."

I turn to him, wishing like hell I could take away every ounce of his suffering. "I know."

We're only on the road for a few hours when I glance in the rearview mirror and notice the sweat beading along Johnny's brow.

I look over my shoulder, confirming my suspicions. I try to reach back and feel for him myself, but I struggle to crane my arm all the way. I let out a breath, gripping the steering wheel and focusing ahead on the signs we pass.

There isn't another rest stop for almost fifty miles, and we're pretty much in the middle of fucking nowhere. A few cars litter the highway going in each direction, but otherwise, it's fairly empty. A whoosh of air hits the side of Beth's bright red BMW, throwing my attention to the semi that's passing us in the left lane.

Once it's just a blur in the distance, I check behind us again. Not a pair of headlights in sight, only a little bit of illumination from our own rear-end on the road.

We're eighty-three miles from our first stop, but with the uncertainty of Johnny's health, I find myself slowing down, signaling, and pulling off onto the shoulder. I make sure to get as far to the right as I can without going too much in the grass along the road. I push the button to put the sports car in park and reposition myself in the seat to take a better look.

Johnny stirs, but otherwise doesn't wake up. There's a pained expression on his face, one that I'd give anything to erase.

I carefully rest the back of my hand against his forehead, noting the damp warmth of his skin. I shift my body around to the front, poking a few things on the dash to get the air conditioning flowing toward him. I reach around, pointing the vents at him, and hope the cool air will ease his discomfort.

He mumbles something under his breath, and his eyes flutter open. His pupils take a second to adjust to the darkness and settle on me. "Claire, what's wrong?" His voice cracks, and he struggles to sit up.

"Shh, it's okay. Stay down." My intentions weren't to wake him, but to make sure he was okay. This entire thing is uncharted territory to me, and I'd be lying if I said I wasn't scared to make a mistake and put him in any more danger than he already is.

"Are we there?" He blinks through the dark.

"No." I shake my head. "You were...I thought you were running a fever."

Why am I so ashamed of being worried about him? Maybe it's because every single little thing out of place sets me on edge. It's difficult to determine which threats are worthy of our attention or not.

Johnny wipes at his brow, a bit of his own embarrassment settling in his features. "I'm fine."

We're on opposite ends of the spectrum—me overly concerned and him blowing things off completely. There needs to be some kind of balance between us, so we don't overlook something that is an actual concern.

"Really." He throws the cover off of him and sits up in the small back seat. Johnny holds his stomach, desperately hiding the twisting of his face.

I grab the bottle of water from the front cup holder and hand it to him. "Will you at least hydrate and take some meds?"

"If that'll get us back on the road."

Although I can pretty much tell that he knows he needs some reprieve from the damage to his body, he's been adamant about consuming the least amount of painkillers he could, and if I didn't push him, he probably wouldn't take any at all. Must be some kind of pride thing. Which makes no sense—he was shot, almost died, and instead of receiving normal medical care, he's being bumped and tossed around in the back seat of a tiny car while he flees across the country to escape the man who wants him dead. It's safe to say he's more than deserving of a couple pills to ease the pain.

But I let him pretend it's all me, if that's what I have to do to get them down his throat.

"Yes." I hand him two small, round tablets. "Thank you."

He swallows them down with a gulp of water and chugs down a bit more.

I hide the smile from forming on my face at correctly guessing he was thirsty.

This man can be completely selfless and do everything for anyone else, but when it comes to tending to himself, he's a lost cause. That's where I come into play. I will pick up the slack and look out for him the same he does for others. Because someone so noble deserves care and consideration, too.

The drugs might be a temporary fix, but it'll buy us a little time until we can get further down the road and to our first stop, where Johnny will get checked over by one of the few physicians we're scheduled to see along the way. It's not an ideal situation, but we're doing the best we can under our fairly shitty circumstances.

Regardless, I'm grateful for the opportunity, considering Johnny could very well have died the way Franklin intended.

JOHNNY – 9

ALMOST TWO MONTHS AGO

"Are you sure you'll still love me?" I ask Claire, the device held tightly in my grasp.

When did I become so fucking insecure all of a sudden?

It's just hair.

Maybe I'm more attached to it than she is.

Claire deadpans. "Seriously?"

I shrug and stare into the mirror of our new apartment. It's not as nice as I'd hoped—the apartment, not the mirror—but the best I could do given our pressing situation. Now that we're here, on the East Coast, I can dig around to see if I can find us something better. Something safer, and a bit more comfortable than the cramped studio space.

I haven't left in the week that we've been here, but with the rest that Claire has sort of forced on me, I've garnered enough strength to finally do the thing I need to do before I can go out in public, even if it is only for very brief blips of time—like running necessary errands or going to get medical attention.

Faking my death means a new identity, and a different appearance. There's only so much I can change, but my signature long locks are a definite sacrifice I have to make. A piece of me that I weirdly hate giving up.

"What if you're not attracted to me anymore?" I meet her gaze in the reflection, her blue eyes staring seriously at me.

"I could shave mine, too, if you're worried." She holds her hair down and tilts her head around to get a better look. "Not sure I could pull it off though."

I turn around to face her. "You wouldn't."

She reaches for the clippers, a devious grin settling into her features. "Dare me?" Claire grabs hold of them and points them toward me. "You want me to do it?"

My eyes widen. "No."

Claire smiles. "I mean yours, not mine."

"Oh." My accelerated pulse starts to slow. It's not that Claire wouldn't still be smoking hot, it's that I'd hate for her to have to give up anything else for me. To be in my life. She's already surrendered more than her fair share at the cost of being with me.

"Let me prove you wrong," she tells me, a softness floating about her voice.

I swallow and nod. "Okay."

Claire flips the switch to the on position, and with a steady humming buzz, she swipes the first section of my hair off.

It lands in a heap on the counter, and she goes in for another. She carefully eyes each one, removing the thick mop on my head.

"Turn around," she tells me.

I face the mirror again, my gaze trailing slowly up to take myself in for the first time with this new look. It's still me, just different. But isn't that the point? It's not like I haven't already changed with everything that's already happened.

Claire stands taller to reach the back of my head. A few buzzes later and she stops, flicking the switch at the same time.

The quiet bathroom dances with my anxious energy.

I remove the white towel around my shoulders and toss it onto the counter. I run my hand through my short spiky hair, noticing a few uneven patches that I'll have to touch up. I fucking hate the way it feels, not because of the job Claire did, but because it's foreign. I'd gotten used to having long hair, running my fingers through like a nervous tick. Now it's bristly and unfamiliar, and I hate how exposed it makes me feel.

Claire presses her body against my back and rests her head along my side. "I'd still do ya."

Despite every terrible thing that's happened, that girl never fails to make me smile.

"Yeah?" I raise an eyebrow at her in the reflection and turn to face her.

She looks up at me, her eyes twinkling. "Mmhm." Claire reaches up and runs her hand across my cheek, settling it against my neck.

I wrap my arm around her waist and pull her up toward me. I'm not supposed to be lifting anything in my condition but screw the doctor's orders—I need to kiss my lady.

Claire kisses me back, tender and soft like she's afraid I might break. Her tongue darts into my mouth, her body reacting in succession to mine.

We haven't shared an intimate moment like this since we've been here, and it's showing through the heated passion that sparks at our touch.

"Johnny," she breathes into my mouth. "We can't."

But it doesn't matter; we can't stop what we already started. Not when it tastes this fucking sweet.

I run my hands down her frame, relishing every curve. I weave them under her shirt, allowing my skin to touch hers. It's smooth and everything I remember it to be.

It's not that we haven't been close since the attack on my life, but we've avoided anything that would exert too much of my energy and potentially hinder my healing. We sleep practically naked together every night, but this is the first time in a while we've let ourselves explore each other this way.

And damn if my entire being doesn't want more, more, more.

"Yes, we can," I tell her, grabbing her by the waist and leading her from our tiny bathroom into the open area that makes up our living space. "I hate how small this place is."

"What? Really? It's cozy."

I break away from her kiss and shove her onto the mattress, dropping to my knees in front of her and immediately finding the button of her pants. I drag them over her ass, wiggling them all of the way off her body and tossing them aside. I climb my way up, dragging my bottom lip along her thigh and tugging at her panties with my teeth.

I fight the breath that catches in my chest. We've barely gotten started, and somehow, I'm already winded. I refuse to allow my lack of endurance to stop us from crossing the finish line.

Claire senses my hesitation and props herself onto her elbows. "Johnny…"

I ignore her, wiggling my finger under the band of her undies and moving them to the side. Gliding my tongue over the remnants of a faded tan line, I make my way to her slit, where I allow myself a taste of her, my cock throbbing in response to her delectable sweetness. I trail down, savoring more of her.

She's wet, so fucking wet, like she's been ready for me this entire time.

I steady myself, trying to even out my ragged breathing in a desperate attempt to play it off like this is no big deal. But if I'm being honest, even if I wasn't recovering from a gunshot wound to the abdomen, I'd still be worked up from waiting this long to be close with the woman I love.

Claire sits up completely, severing the connection between me and her sugary bits.

I sigh. "I'm fine."

"You don't sound fine." She wipes at my lip with her thumb. "I don't want to hurt you."

Is this how she feels when I treat her exactly the same? How do I prove to her that I want this despite the danger it potentially poses?

"You're not hurting me." *Unless you count my pounding boner.* "I want this."

Claire's blue gaze scans my face.

I know she's struggling between being safe and frantically wanting this, too.

"Lay down," she demands. "I'm doing the work." Claire places her hands on my shoulders and guides me onto my back.

My heart picks up its pace, and I do my best to hide my triumphant grin.

Claire glides her hands to my waist, tugging my boxers and gray sweats over my hips in one solid motion, freeing my erection in the process. She brings her face to my dick, blowing a bit of cool air along the shaft before running her tongue teasingly over the base and up to swirl around the top.

I flop my head against the bed, my eyes practically rolling back as she licks the precum and spreads her lips around my cock. She takes me into her mouth, sliding it deep into the back of her throat. I throb against her teeth and revel in the pleasure it brings me.

Knowing how much I'm fucking loving this, she giggles and pulls away. She straddles my waist, teasing us both as she glides herself over me and reaches for a condom from the nightstand next to the bed. Claire finds one in my wallet, pulling it out and tossing the rest aside. She brings the package to her mouth and bites the corner off.

Who would have known using protection could be so fucking hot?

Claire pulls the rubber out, immediately moving to secure it around my ready member. Within seconds, she's positioned herself in place, sliding herself over me to continue this whirlwind of pleasure.

My wound tugs, a dull pain, reminding me that this is far from what we should be doing, but I ignore it and focus on the beautiful woman riding my cock.

Claire swivels up and down, her pussy tightening and telling me just where she is on her ascent to climax. One thing is for sure, in all the time Claire and I spent together prior to taking a break from sexual activities, I got very acquainted with her body and the way it ebbs and flows.

She brings her face to mine, kissing me with a feverish intensity.

I fight to pace myself, to revel in experiencing this fleeting moment with her.

Claire rocks herself steadily into me, shortening the strides but thrusting them deeper.

I run my tongue along her bottom lip and drag it into my mouth with my teeth, nibbling and sucking at it gently.

She reacts by digging her hands into the sheets near my head, getting a better grip to push herself into me. She lets out a soft moan, the sound fluttering straight to my cock.

"Together?" Claire breathes into me.

"Together," I mutter in response, grabbing her ass and taking over our rhythm, sending her spiraling around me the second I take control.

I explode inside of her, a wave of both pleasure and pain rippling through my body. Somehow the mixture of the two intensifies the sensation, and I welcome it all.

A perfect depiction of our lives together: so much darkness, yet so much fucking light.

CLAIRE – 10

NOW

This past week has been strange.

Griffin is dead. And while that may be great news, considering what I did to ensure that happened, there's still the possibility that the poison I put into Griffin's mouth will show up during his autopsy, giving away the fact that he didn't actually die of complications from his accident.

That it was me that killed him.

I killed someone. On purpose.

Without so much as a second thought.

And not for one moment have I ever regretted it. The only thing that concerns me is getting caught—and what Johnny would think of me if he knew the truth.

He looks at me like I'm this sweet and innocent person, a fragile, delicate being. Would he run the other way if he found out what I did to rid Griffin from my life?

Even in death, he's still a lingering presence, threatening to ruin everything Johnny and I have worked so hard for.

I thought I was doing the right thing, to eliminate Griffin completely, but what if I made things worse by taking matters into my own hands? What if my actions are unforgivable in Johnny's eyes?

All I wanted was to take back the control Griffin had stolen from me so long ago.

Despite all of my worries, Johnny has somehow been sweeter than usual. If that's even possible. With me, he's this gentle, kind man, but with everyone else, he's cold and shut off, sometimes harsh. I'm the only one who gets to see his soft side, and I'm not mad about that one bit. I love that Johnny is comfortable enough with me to open up, to give me his heart and soul. But what if I don't deserve that?

Especially with the enormous secret I'm keeping from him. Along with the fact that I may have fibbed about needing a cheek swab for food allergies, when in reality it was for an ancestry test to see if he has any living family members.

The results of which happen to be coming in today.

Johnny wraps his arms around my waist and hugs me from behind. He buries his face in my hair and kisses my neck. "I'm going to miss you."

I hold him tightly and cherish the warmth that settles throughout my soul with his touch. I lean into him and sigh. "I wish you could come with me." I turn so I'm facing him, his hands still gripping my middle. "Maybe soon? Now that your I.D. came in?" I run my thumb along his bushy eyebrow and along his cheek. I'll never quite get used to how good-looking he is. Those emerald eyes shining against his long, dark lashes that any girl would pay a lot of money to have.

Johnny leans forward, running his nose along mine. Gently, he presses his mouth against my bottom lip. "Maybe."

I kiss him and cherish the sweet and savory taste of him. My tongue darts out, dancing elegantly with his. No matter how much time passes, I can never quite get used to the fluttering that appears with his touch. There's so much of us that fits perfectly together. Both physically and spiritually—as if we were once one soul, split in two, only to find each other again.

It's crazy to think that we've known each other less than a year, when it feels like we've been together since the beginning of time. Life before Johnny is a blur, and life without him, well, that seems completely unthinkable.

"As much as I want you to stay..." Johnny breathes into me, his fingers gripping me tighter. "You're going to be late."

I glance across at the clock on the microwave. "Shit."

He breaks away, a beautiful grin on his face. Johnny snatches my backpack from the dining room chair and hands it to me. "Here." He plants one final kiss on my cheek.

In a perfect world, Johnny would be coming with me. He'd be attending classes and taking the steps he needed to pursue whatever path he wanted. He'd hold my hand and walk me to our car, open my door and drive the couple blocks to our school. We'd meet each other outside of our classes when they let out and be a normal college couple.

But instead, I drive the short distance to campus alone, my only company the endless thoughts that float in and out of my head. Luckily, Rosie is there to greet me when I park, helping to distract me a little from my chaotic mind.

It's been wonderful to have her around, although she's only been informed of bits and pieces of the situation. Johnny and I already feel guilty about getting her involved, but considering she's my very best friend, there was no way I could go on without her in some capacity.

Rosie has actually been incredibly accommodating, given our super-secretive nature. Don't get me wrong, she's definitely tried to ask questions and get more details, but she's never once faltered or judged us for the weirdness of everything.

I guess when you've been friends with someone for so long, you roll with the punches when shit hits the fan.

"How was your date?" I ask her, happy to take my thoughts

away from my own drama. It's only a matter of minutes until I find out the results of Johnny's ancestry test, and if I don't focus on something else, I may lose my mind.

Rosie rolls her eyes and shakes her head. "Terrible. I'm telling you, the dating pool is absolute garbage. Not only was the guy twenty minutes late, but he also showed up piss drunk."

"You're joking!" I sidestep a pile of slushy snow and continue on our path to the main building.

"I wish I was." Rosie tugs her burgundy scarf closer to her. "I gave him the benefit of the doubt, you know, because I was already there. But then, he proceeded to order himself two shots of tequila, and then had the audacity to say he forgot his wallet."

I gasp and shoot her a look. "You have the worst luck with guys."

"You're telling me."

"I'm sorry, Rose." And I really mean it. Rosie is a catch. She's intelligent, has a great sense of humor, she's driven, and need I mention, gorgeous. She may be my longtime friend, but anyone would be a fool not to recognize how much she has to offer.

"Not your fault." She opens up the door to our classroom and holds it for me to enter. "I'm meeting another guy tonight; fingers crossed it goes better. From his profile, he seems decent, but I've been fooled before."

"I'm rooting for you." I give her a smile and walk over to the table we've claimed as our own since school has started.

"Specifically doing a coffee date. Not giving him an opportunity to get drunk. I swear, this shit is like trial and error." She settles into her seat. "You're lucky you found what you did with JJ."

I sigh, my heart fluttering at the thought of Johnny. I am fortunate to have him in my life. But our journey has been nothing easy. We've had to fight tooth and nail, risking it all on numerous occasions to keep ourselves and our love alive. Our bond is strong and unbreakable, but the things we've had to overcome, I wouldn't wish that on anyone else.

"Class, the results are in." Professor Adkins strolls into the room, holding a stack of envelopes in his hand. "To get yours, you must turn in your assignment that was due today."

A few students in the corner groan, clearly letting the rest of us know that they haven't finished their paper yet.

"Those of you who are actually doing the work I assign, you can grab yours and head to the computer lab down the hall to access the records." The professor looks right at me. "Those of you who submitted more than one, make sure you pay the extra fee prior to pick up."

A fifty-dollar charge that I used out of my own funds. Johnny wouldn't have batted an eye about the amount, but I didn't want to involve him anymore in this lie than I already had.

Rosie and I make our way to the front of the room, our papers in hand, ready to exchange for the packages containing details about us that we're unaware of. Even Rosie doesn't know much about her ancestry outside of her grandparents on her mom's side.

"Ms. Cooper." Adkins nods and gives me two envelopes.

I swallow down the uncertainty that rises from the forbidden weight resting in my grasp. In a matter of moments, I'll know more about Johnny's past than he does, and I'm not sure if that will be a good or a bad thing. I hope like hell there's some kind of silver lining that will come from me going behind his back. He has me, but I don't want him to be alone in this world. No one deserves that. Well, not including Griffin or Franklin—they both deserve to spend an eternity alone.

"You okay?" Rosie asks me.

I walk toward the door. "Yeah." I nod to her own envelope. "You're not worried?"

She shrugs and briefly glances at it. "Not really. Be cool to be related to someone famous though. Maybe royalty or something. I'm pretty sure I'm a mutt. I doubt there will be any big surprises."

I probably am, too, but it's not my results that have me flustered. It's Johnny's.

Now, with the way things are, there are so many possibilities. But with this information, it will solidify whether or not Johnny has anyone else in his family tree still alive. And I'm not sure if I can handle knowing the truth if it's bad news. I'm already keeping too much from him, how can I withhold that, too? I'll have to come clean, about this, and about everything, if we stand any chance of making it through these dark days.

We've already overcome so much, we can get through this, too, right?

I follow Rosie into the room and claim the computer next to her. The screen glares back at me, that cursor button blinking and waiting for me to make my move.

"Here, let me." Rosie reaches over me and types in the domain and hits enter. Her blonde hair wafts strawberries as it passes my face. She pokes at the page she pulled out of her envelope. "Looks like you just enter your code into there." Rosie points at the screen. "Whose are you going to do first?"

I avert my gaze, glaring at the two packages in front of me. "Um."

Rosie punches in her details and waits for her results to load. They're there within seconds. Her past and present right there for her to consume.

I slide my finger under the paper to break the seal, revealing a set of log-in instructions. Without allowing myself the chance to back out, I key the information into the browser quickly. I hover over the submit button as the severity of the situation comes around full force. Holding my breath, I push it anyway.

All too fast and too slow, the page loads, showing me more than I could have bargained for.

My heart pounds wildly as my eyes scan everything in front of me.

Genetic Ancestry.
DNA Matches.
DNA Circles.

I immediately click on the matches, frantic to finally satiate the burning desire to know the truth.

Only, the moment my gaze settles, my stomach clenches, my mouth dropping open.

"What's wrong?" Rosie asks me.

I blink twice, thinking I'm not possibly seeing clearly. I look again, sure that I'm reading this all wrong.

Lynne Jones, mother, deceased.

A piece of information I already knew. Johnny's late mother, who died when he was young. He barely speaks of her, but when he does, I can tell it pains him to relive the memory of her.

It's not his mom that unsettles me, though. It's the next line down.

"It's..." but I can't finish my sentence. It would make it all too real.

Luciano Bane, father.

But that's it. No deceased. No nothing. Just his name.

Meaning, his father is very much alive.

A father he has no idea even exists, let alone is still out there.

Here I was thinking I was going to find some long-lost grandparent or uncle, but I ended up with the name of his biological father. And I'm not entirely sure if that's good or bad. Clearly, this guy played no active role in Johnny's life, so maybe telling Johnny he's still out there would hurt him more, knowing he's alive and could have reached out, but never did.

I pull up a second browser, desperate to find out more information about this mystery man whose sole part in the creation of Johnny was as a sperm donor. Almost like what my mother had been for me, a vessel to bring me into this world, only to leave me once I was born.

I type in the name, noticing the Google search bar trying to complete my request.

Luciano Bane net worth.

Luciano Bane possible murder.

Luciano Bane owner of Bane Café.

Luciano Bane crimes.

Is it possible there's another person out there with the same name drawing this attention?

But, when I click enter and the first photo pops up, it's like I'm staring at Johnny, only he's aged, with a full, clean-cut beard, and there's a sort of darkness to him that my Johnny doesn't have. The resemblance is uncanny, almost like you put Johnny in one of those age simulators to show how he would look at the age of forty-something.

There's no denying that this man, this potential criminal, is Johnny's father.

Here I thought I was doing the right thing, but I may have just opened up a can of worms that can't be closed. I wanted to find a sweet old grandparent who could share their recipes and family photos, not add another layer of negativity to Johnny's life.

Rosie cranes her neck to check out my screen. She lowers her voice. "Is that who I think it is?"

I bite my lip and barely bob my head up and down, letting my eyes scan the news articles. My sights land on one from a local gossip paper. Dated only a few months back.

Possible Crime Syndicate Permanently Relocates.

I skim the details, my breath catching when I realize what exactly this means.

Not only is Johnny's dad alive, and into some bad stuff, but he likely lives within a few miles of us.

I sink back into my seat and let the weight of it all crash over me.

Rosie tightens her high ponytail. "What are you going to do?"

"What *should* I do?"

Tell him, my mind urges me.

But what if that's the wrong choice? Johnny already has enough on his plate, what if this sets him over the edge? Not only will he be upset that I went behind his back, but then knowing his dad is out there, and that he's a criminal on top of it? And there's still the truth of the Griffin situation. All of these secrets are piling up and building a wedge between us. I can't allow this to be what breaks us, though. We've been through more than our fair share, but what if this is too much? There has to be some kind of breaking point—something that we can't come back from.

Why did I ever think this would be a good idea? The way everything else has gone for us, I should have known this would result in nothing but disappointment.

"That's up to you," Rosie tells me. "How do you think he'll handle it?"

I scan the screen once more, sighing at the mess this man has gotten himself into. If these reports are correct, Luciano is basically the Franklin of the east coast. And knowing what Franklin has done to us, and countless others, there's no telling how Johnny will react.

"I don't know," I say honestly.

Johnny may have gotten wrapped up in some bad shit, but not for a second did he do so selfishly. Every single thing he's done has been for the sake of saving someone else. He's sacrificed himself time and time again to do the right thing, the noble thing. Johnny is a good man, one this world doesn't deserve. And here he is, bred from a criminal and a woman who ultimately went down bad path after bad path until she met her untimely demise. It would crush him to know what a bad man his father is. What if he loses himself thinking that he's going down that same road?

I can see Johnny's true self. The good one. But all he notices when he looks in the mirror is a bad guy. The one who's done terrible things. He doesn't believe he's worthy of anything good, or to be loved, when in reality, he's the best person I've ever known. Anyone who ever took a second to truly get to know him would say the same damn thing.

Even in the beginning, when Johnny partially had me fooled, Bram tried to convince me otherwise. Because Bram knew the truth. Johnny is a sheep in wolf's clothing. Don't get me wrong—he's fierce and intimidating, but it's only when those he cares about are in danger. He would risk anything to save someone who needed rescuing. And that's the difference between Johnny and everyone he's interacted with during his journey to the underworld.

"I'm going to find him." The words that leave my mouth surprise even me.

Rosie's eyes go wide. "What?"

"I have to. I have to see it for myself. I can't get Johnny involved until I know." Just as Johnny would do for me, I will do what I can to protect him. It's my fault I dug too deep, and now I will be the one to handle what comes from it.

JOHNNY - 11

I hate it when Claire is gone.

This world is too dangerous to not worry my ass off every second she's away. I try to distract myself, following up on leads of where Franklin might be, keeping tabs on his whereabouts and his moves to note anything suspicious. But no matter what, my mind always floats back to her dark, honey-colored hair and bright blue eyes.

It's been a week since we heard the news of Griffin's death, and somehow, Claire has stayed with me. I keep waiting for her to realize that I'm a monster—a killer—but she doesn't. She hasn't even brought it up, which is equal parts relief and a concern.

I don't want her to suppress her feelings because she's afraid of being honest with me. I want her to be able to talk to me, even when it's uncomfortable. We're a team, and there isn't anything we can't handle together. Never do I want her to feel like she can't tell me something. I'd never judge her or try to gaslight her out of feeling a certain way. She matters to me, more than I'll ever fully comprehend, and I hope that she knows I'm here for her through it all—whatever life throws our way.

And if not being with me is what she truly wants, I will respect that, despite it being the most painful thing I can imagine.

Even worse than death itself.

And trust me, I've been pretty fucking close to knowing what that's like.

I wouldn't blame her for walking away. How could I expect her to understand that I did what I did to protect her? That everything I've ever done was because I thought it was the right thing to do. But why do I get to choose what's right or wrong? How do my bad actions get somehow justified based on my personal rationale?

I shake the thought and walk down the steps and into the front lobby of our building. I nod a hello to the kind-looking older woman picking up her tiny dog to carry it up the stairs. Walking out the main doors, the crisp cold air rushes to greet me, reminding me there are still a few more months until spring arrives, another season I'm curious to experience from the East Coast's perspective.

I glance left, then right, and cross the not very busy street, making my way to the post office to check our mailbox. Claire is still anxious about her scholarship details coming in, so I'm making sure to check daily in hopes that the letter will arrive and ease her nerves. No matter how many times I've told her that money is no issue, she hasn't let up with wanting to cover her tuition herself.

Just the thought of her brings a smile to my face. I can't exactly blame her for her rationale, I would probably be the same exact way if the situation were reversed. She's honestly handling it all better than I thought she would. Claire has been nothing but a wonderful surprise from day one, and I can only imagine that will continue with each moment spent together.

"Johnny?" A thick, familiar voice stops me dead in my tracks.

My heart clenches. I will myself to become invisible but it's no use.

Other than Claire and Rosie, no one, and I mean no one, should know my name out here.

I swallow. I could easily ignore the person, keep moving and pretend I didn't hear them. I could act like I'm tying my shoe, which would explain why I suddenly stopped. Or I could turn and face the person that voice came from.

"Johnny?" The person calls out again, this time a little closer.

My window of escape is closing. I've tried like hell to prepare myself for something like this, but I guess I always expected Franklin to be the one to come for me, not the man stepping around me to stand in front of me.

The guy I trusted, probably more than I should.

I raise my gaze from the ground ahead and up to meet his wild stare. "Josey."

He clutches his chest. "Holy shit." Josey steps forward, but I take one back. "Dude, seriously?" He closes the gap anyway, wrapping his wide arms around me, surprising me when he hugs me tight. "I thought you were fucking dead."

With my arms pinned to my side in a Josey hug, I mutter back, "Yeah, that was the whole point."

Josey lets go and clamps my shoulders. He grips me firmly and takes a solid look at me. "I can't believe it." He punches my arm. "Here you are, in the fucking flesh."

My attention darts all around, looking for some kind of exit. It's Josey, and although he's someone I once believed in, he could be here on behalf of Franklin to finish the job he had started back on the west coast.

"I heard rumors, man, I had to come see it for myself." Josey shakes his head. "You couldn't have picked some place a little warmer?" He rubs his arms. "It's frigid as fuck here." Josey kicks at a little pile of snow on the ground. "Even this shit is ugly."

Despite the raging panic coursing through me, it's strangely liberating to see him. We grew close in our time together, and I hated not being able to tell him the truth. But I couldn't risk

Franklin finding out, not just for my sake, but for Claire's, too. Honestly, I'm not sure I would have made it this far without Josey and the tip he gave me about that package being stolen from me being an inside job. Without that information, I might not have ever tracked it down and bought myself more time with Franklin. Josey risked his ass to help me out, which should show me where his loyalties lie. But one can never be too sure, especially in our line of business.

"Does anyone know you're here?" I ask the question that's nagging me.

Josey straightens up, easily towering over me with his height and build. Josey is a large dude. Someone I definitely wouldn't want to get into a fistfight with. "Told them I had some family business to attend to." He clears his throat. "I really do, my gran is sick."

"Ah, shit, Jose, I'm sorry, man." This time, it's me that slaps his shoulder.

It's like we're brought back to those nights behind Franklin's place. A difficult, but much simpler time. One when I wasn't running for my life, just running illegal packages all over the city.

"She's lived a long life." Josey sniffles and rubs his nose. "Anyway, no, boss didn't send me, if that's what you're wondering. But I wouldn't be surprised if he does come after you soon. Word on the streets is he might be putting a bounty on you. You really got under his skin, JJ."

I let out a nervous laugh. "What's stopping him then?"

Josey scratches his temple. "If I had to guess, I'd say it's because he wants to do it himself."

At least I was right about one thing—Franklin wants to be the one to finish me off.

It's probably a good thing I've gotten under his skin like I have, otherwise he would have just paid someone to end this weeks ago.

"Well, thanks for the warning?" I glance around at the oncoming passersby, scanning them for any kind of immediate threat.

They might not be there to kill me, but he could easily have someone capture and hold me captive until he got here to follow through with killing me.

"Had to see you for myself." Josey stares at me with such intensity. "I've got to say, man, you did a damn good job. You had everyone fooled." He chuckles. "Claire slapped the shit out of me at your funeral. She was pissed. Not that I blame her. I would have decked myself, too."

"What gave it away?" I've done everything I can to cover my tracks.

"Facial recognition shit. Some college kid posted you in the back of his Instagram story." He glances around, too. "Umm, Pax? Does that ring a bell?"

I knew I hated that guy for a reason. Had to have been the first time we hung out with Claire's friends, before we thoroughly enforced the no social media rule. He was live streaming and panned all around him, managing to clip part of my face before I realized what was happening. I turned as quickly as I could, but it must have been *just* enough to set Franklin off.

A chill creeps up my spine. He must have eyes reaching further than I thought he did.

Or, he's monitoring anyone Claire has ever been associated with, in case we slip up.

It was one time, and only for the briefest moment, but it was enough to cause Franklin to be suspicious of my death.

"How much time do you think I have?"

Josey shrugs. "Not sure, kid. He has some more pressing business he's taking care of, but probably another few weeks at max."

"Damn, okay." I take his words in, letting them be fully absorbed.

How in the hell am I going to weasel my way out of this mess? I thought I had escaped Franklin's wrath, but I only bought myself time. Time I haven't fully utilized, considering he could be coming after me at any moment. How does someone even go about getting out of something like this?

The only possible solution I can come up with is ending Franklin's life.

There's no other option. He's a man that can't be reasoned with. And at this point, killing me will be more satisfying than anything I could ever offer him. There's no chance I'd ever go back to working for him, because he'd only continue to put my life in danger until there was another *accident.* Not to mention, I'd never put Claire in that kind of danger.

But if I take Franklin out of the equation, what would happen next? Would someone replace him and want revenge? I may have worked for him, but I don't know enough about his organization to have the ins and outs of that type of system. The main reason I got to live as long as I did was because of his wife—does that mean she would be the one to take over once he's gone?

And how could I even begin to put myself in the position to kill him? He'd never be stupid enough to come at me unarmed or without guards.

I pull the buzzing phone out of my pocket.

Claire: Me & Rose are going to grab coffee. I'll be a little late, love you.

Me: Be safe, please. Love you more.

Usually, this is where I would ask Claire where she's going and have her keep me posted when she gets there, but Josey is standing in front of me, telling me I only have a few weeks to live. Claire only just got her life back; I don't want to ruin it already. I'll try to preserve what little bit of normalcy she has left for as long as I can.

"What can I do to help?" Josey surprises me with his question.

His expression is stern, showing nothing but candor.

"What?" I can't hide the surprise in my tone.

"Dude, I thought you were dead once, I think I'll pass on the real thing." Josey crosses his arms over his broad chest. "Listen, man, I didn't get the chance to warn you last time, and that shit ate me alive."

Ah, so Josey is here because he feels guilty. He's trying to clear his conscience.

"You're not a bad guy, JJ. And maybe not everyone sees that, but I do. I'm not trying to get all sentimental...but you're like the kid brother I never had."

Or maybe he's here because he actually cares.

I narrow my eyes at him. "Are you fucking with me?"

Josey grins and shakes his head. "I'm serious, you fucking idiot." He punches my shoulder. "I'm only in town for another week, but if you need me, I'm here."

I sigh and glance around, my breath a misty haze in front of me. Having someone other than Claire on my team would be huge, especially since I don't want to involve her just yet. But what if this is a trick? What if Josey really is a mole for Franklin, and he's using what connection we did have as a way to trap me? If it were only me, I would take Josey up on his offer of assistance without hesitation, but I have to give more caution to things involving Claire.

I would never forgive myself if something happened to her and I could have prevented it.

"Thanks, man," I finally say. I reach out my hand, letting it hang in the balance between us. "I'll let you know."

Josey rolls his eyes, which is hilarious coming from such a large and intimidating man. He grabs my outreached arm and pulls me to him, slapping my back in a manly kind of hug. "I'm glad you're not dead, kid."

I smile and smack him with the same intensity. "Me too, me too."

"If you need me, I'll be at a place called Bane's Café at noon every day."

And maybe it's foolish of me, but I make a mental note of the location. I have no idea what I'm going to do to make it out of this, and if it's a trap, I'll be walking right into it. Josey has already proven himself on more than one occasion, what's the harm in putting a little faith in him once again?

CLAIRE – 12

I drive the three blocks from campus and park across the street from my destination.

It's eerily similar to Bram's, with the glowing signage out front and the large windowpane that shows the contents of the diner. Immediately, I'm taken back to the aroma of freshly brewed coffee and blueberry muffins. That home away from home feeling that cascaded over me the second I stepped foot into Bram's diner.

I hadn't been out west long, but I grew attached to that place and the man with salt and pepper hair and advice that was almost always on point. He was like a fairy-godfather, one that I would love to consult with on what the heck to do with this new information I've learned about Johnny's past.

I smile, thinking of Bram playing matchmaker with me and Johnny when we were in the *avoiding each other like the plague* stage of our relationship. The look on Bram's face when we finally started getting along was priceless, like he had hit the lottery. He looked out for Johnny as if he was his own flesh and blood, and I admired how much the two of them cared for one another.

Just goes to show you that sometimes the best family is found.

Which brings me to sitting in front of this knock-off Bram's, squinting my eyes to get a better look from my spot tucked carefully in my car.

I really could use a cup of coffee, so what's the harm in wandering inside for one?

I swallow down the nerves building up and do exactly that, hitting the lock button on my key fob and crossing the relatively empty street.

How have I lived here my entire life but never visited this specific coffee shop? Maybe because it's not within a walking distance of my house, and until recently, I've done the majority of my traversing on foot.

"Welcome to Bane's," a friendly, teenaged girl with rosy cheeks greets me.

A barista pulls a shot of espresso, and a middle-aged woman sits in the corner, tapping away on the keys of her laptop.

Taking everything in, I stroll toward the ordering area, where a large chalkboard has the menu listed. I study it over, out of curiosity more than anything.

"What can I get for you?" It's another teenager, this one with a beanie on his head and a sad attempt at a mustache hovering above his lip.

"Coffee, black. Please."

The kid blinks at me, like he's waiting for me to rattle the variations of milk and syrups I'd like to include with my order.

"With a dash of cinnamon."

"That's it?" He seems stunned by my sort of simple order.

"Yep."

He pushes a few buttons on his screen. "For here or to go?"

I bite at my lip, knowing damn well I should leave, but the nosiness in me not letting me go that easily. "For here, please."

"Miller," a deep voice calls out from the back.

The cashier turns his head to glance behind him. "Sir?"

My heart nearly drops when the man comes out. Dark, bushy hair with a hint of silver poking through. Bright emerald eyes and long, long lashes. He's easily six foot something, with a wide but not too big of a build. Intimidating to say the very least.

The man catches me staring at him and he pauses. "Sorry, I didn't realize you were with a customer, carry on."

Manners? From a potential mob boss? At this point, I wouldn't be surprised if he sprouted a tail or set of wings and flew away.

Miller gives me his attention once again. "That'll be three dollars."

I slide him a five, take my change from him, and end up handing him a single back.

The kid offers me a smile. "Thanks." He turns around, grabbing a cup and a saucer from the stack by the kitchen window and setting it in front of me.

The man waits patiently for Miller to finish, and I do my best to avoid making eye contact with him. I thought maybe I would catch a glimpse of him, not be gawked at for minutes on end.

"Here you go." Miller sets the cinnamon shaker next to my steaming cup.

"That's how I take mine," the man says with a grin, stepping forward.

My pulse thuds loudly in my ears, and I do everything I can to stay firmly in place and not turn and run out of here. I never meant to garner *this much* attention from the guy I came here in search of.

I note the way his lips turn up: the same exact way Johnny's do when he's trying to hide his smile. The similarities between the two of them are eerie, confirming my suspicions of whether or not the results of the ancestry kit were accurate.

"Yeah?" I finally say.

"Mmhm. Adds just the right amount of flare without being too much." He points to the glass case of sweets. "Could I offer you something to go with your coffee? A muffin maybe?"

I eye the case but shake my head. "No, thank you though, I appreciate it."

"I insist." He turns to Miller. "Bag up a blueberry old-fashioned for the lady." He winks at me. "I saw the way you hesitated." He takes the thing from Miller and sets it on the counter by my cup. "It's my favorite, too."

I dig my teeth into the inside of my lip to ground myself from losing control. Never could I have ever imagined *this* is how this entire interaction would go.

The man who looks just like an older version of the love of my life extends his hand. "Luciano."

I wipe my clammy palm on my pants and take his in mine. "Claire." It's not until the word slips from my lips that I realize I probably should have used a fake one. Now I've given him a piece of me that I can never take back.

Johnny is going to be so fucking mad when he finds out. And I don't blame him one bit.

This is stupid, completely foolish and irresponsible.

"Claire," Luciano repeats. "What a lovely name."

But there's something laced in his tone, something dangerous that sends a chill dancing up my spine.

His grip is firm but gentle, his hand consuming mine almost completely. "I'll leave you to it." Luciano nods toward my steaming cup and turns toward Miller. "There's a shipment in the back I could use your assistance with."

Miller makes eye contact with me and points across the room. "Sorcha can help with anything else."

"Thanks."

The two of them disappear, the door swishing in their wake.

And I'm left here, processing what the fuck just happened.

I came here to see for myself. To see if that man who showed up on Johnny's results was actually his father. To see if he was in fact, the crime boss that the internet claims he is.

I'm not sure what I expected, really. But for him to be so...charismatic...that was a surprise. There were layers of Johnny woven throughout him—in his mannerisms and even the sly twinkle in his eye. There is no denying that this man is his father.

But now, what do I do with that information?

He seems like a decent guy. Someone Johnny might not hate. He's the owner of a quaint corner coffee shop. Similar to his found father figure back home. Although, there's still the very real possibility that he's involved in illegal activities. And I guess that's what I have to figure out. Johnny is finally getting clear of that type of stuff; I won't be the reason he can't escape that lifestyle. He deserves to be free of the shit that wrecked the past year of his life and nearly killed him.

Plus, if he really is Johnny's biological father, he has some explaining to do on where he's been the past twenty years.

I take a sip of my coffee, savoring the bitter taste. If anything, the guy serves a decent cup of joe, giving him at least one brownie point.

I pull my phone out of my pocket, surprised when I don't have any notifications. Usually, Johnny would have followed up by now, but maybe he's busy with something else. I send him a text anyway in an attempt to calm his nerves in case he's trying to give me space.

He's done such a great job at balancing the strangeness of our situation. It's been hard on him, trying to play pretend that everything is fine, but he's gone out of his way to make things as normal as possible despite the raging nerves he deals with daily. He's still worried Franklin will come after him even though it's been months and nothing has happened.

At this point, the biggest concern should be whether or not the poison will show up on Griffin's autopsy.

Me: Coffee is decent, I'll see you soon.
Johnny: I'm glad. You having a good time?

I shouldn't have lied about being with Rosie. I should have told him a partial truth, that I was trying a new café. Or actually brought Rosie with me. The dishonesties add to the weight already pushing down on us.

Me: Yes, just missing you.
Johnny: Me too, always.

There's a sort of comfort to having Johnny around. A safety. A sense of home no matter where I am. Without him, there's this strange absence. Like part of me is missing. It's not that I'm dependent on Johnny, but instead, we somehow make each other stronger. It's difficult to wrap my head around and explain, but it's the only thing I've ever been absolutely certain about.

Johnny is my person. And I am his.

I take a few more swallows of my drink and push the cup forward, dropping my napkin on top. Hopping off the stool, I grab the paper bag with the donut inside and make my way toward the door. Once I'm outside, I exhale, allowing the slightest release of tension from my body.

"Over here," a person calls out from somewhere in the distance.

I turn toward the sound and take a few steps in that direction. A dark alley right behind Bane's Café. Almost immediately, my thoughts are transported to my birthday. That dreadful night where everything was perfect, until it wasn't. When Johnny's life almost slipped completely away from me. When I had been convinced I lost him forever. When a large piece of me was tainted with the thirst for revenge and the need to protect Johnny at all costs.

Watching something terrible happen to someone you love will change you.

With a mind of their own, my feet inch closer to the darkness beyond. It consumes me completely and a strange sort of calm comes over me. The shade a welcomed friend, saying hello to that part of me I try like hell to keep hidden from the world.

I tiptoe further, my back against the brick wall, slithering quietly toward the entrance of the back of the café.

A box van starts its engine, seconds later pulling away, leaving two people behind.

I stay in the shadows, lurking for any sign or clue of what's going on. Is this just an innocent delivery? Or something much more sinister?

"Net twenty thousand," the smaller of the two says.

It's Miller.

My eyes adjust, finally noticing the beanie resting on his head, and the silhouette of Luciano standing in front of him.

"Down ten percent." Luciano seems disappointed. "We'll have to put pressure on the north end if we're going to recoup costs."

"Who do you want to use?" Miller asks him.

"Viktor."

Miller looks up from the clipboard in his hands and stares at Luciano. "Are you sure?"

Luciano nods stiffly. "Yes."

"Okay, sir." Miller's voice cracks.

"Any word yet on what's going on out west?"

"No, sir. Only that it's a personal vendetta."

"Leave it to Franklin to get distracted by such things." Luciano lets out a breath.

And without meaning to, I suck one in. Did he just say what I think he did?

Out west? Franklin? As in the same Franklin we ran away from?

Personal vendetta.

Could he be referring to Johnny? Does that mean Franklin is aware Johnny faked his own death? Or is this all just some weird coincidence that Luciano knows someone by the same name and location?

Luciano shifts his sights from Miller and looks directly at me, squinting to see more clearly.

My eyes go wide and I freeze in place, hoping with all my might that he doesn't see me creeping from the dimness of the alley. I take a cautious step back, the ground betraying me by crackling under my shoe.

Luciano shoves Miller aside, his hand reaching back and resting on his hip as he makes his way toward me. Probably on a gun.

I could run, dart away quickly, but what if he decides to put a bullet in me before I can evade him? I have no option other than to stay put and hope he doesn't shoot me.

What a fucking fool I was—for coming here at all, and especially for thinking I could eavesdrop in a shady alley and not get caught.

I'm smarter than this, so why am I making stupid mistakes?

"Claire?" Luciano narrows his gaze and slowly takes his grip from his side.

"Hey, um, sorry. I thought this connected to Bradley Street." I tilt my head and put on my absolute best lost-ditzy-girl act.

Luciano continues to stare at me, as if determining whether or not he buys my story. "You shouldn't be on this side of town at night. It's dangerous." His voice is gravelly yet calm.

"Right, yeah. I'll just…" I turn toward the light of where I came from, but he reaches out and grabs my arm, stopping me completely.

"Claire." Luciano doesn't break his firm but soft hold.

I yank free of him, just to make sure I can.

He holds both of his palms in the air. "I was going to offer you a ride." Luciano points toward Miller, who stands waiting for Luciano to return. "These streets really aren't the safest."

I rub the spot where his hand once was. "No, I'm fine."

Luciano tilts his head. "Very well. Have a good evening."

"You, too." I waste no more time, making my way from him as quick as I can without raising too much concern at my speed. I feel his eyes on me the entire trek to my car.

I should have continued on foot, long enough to break his attention, but with the uncertainty of the Franklin situation still lingering, it wouldn't be safe to roam around in an area I'm unfamiliar with. I already risked too much by coming here alone, I shouldn't risk anymore.

The comfort of being inside of my car calms me only a little bit. I won't truly feel safe until Johnny is right next to me.

JOHNNY – 13

I can no longer tell the difference between my own paranoia and real life.

Every single thing causes my mind to race.

I fucking hate hiding things from Claire, but I don't want to tell her about the note from Franklin, and Josey showing up, until I actually have some kind of plan put in place to get us out of this mess I've created. I was selfish for allowing Claire to waltz right into this chaos, and I refuse to let her fall victim to something that was my fault.

"What's on your mind?" Claire glances at me in the mirror as she braids her long brown hair.

I let out a breath and take in her beauty. "You're really pretty."

She rolls her eyes and blushes. "That was *not* what was on your mind."

I shrug and lay back on the bed, one arm behind my head, the other resting on my stomach. "Coulda been."

Claire plops down beside me and props herself up on her elbows. "Tell me."

I reach forward to run my fingers down her cheek. "You're beautiful."

"Fine then." She pokes me in the side and laughs. "Secrets don't make friends."

Oh, what I would give to just confess it all. To not harbor a single piece of information that she wasn't aware of. But if I'm going to keep her safe, I have to hold off a little longer. I don't want to ruin her mundane college experience any sooner than I have to. She deserves that, at least.

Her phone buzzes, and when she glances down at it, her eyes go wide. Claire answers it immediately. "Dad?" She presses her index finger to her lips to signal me to be quiet and then clicks the speakerphone button.

"Claire-bear!" The genuine happiness in his tone is heart-warming.

"Hey, Pops." Her eyes glisten with the tears she's holding back. "How's Africa?"

The line cracks slightly. "It's good, but hey, I don't have long, just a few minutes. The international rates are insane, I had to prepay just to make the call. Anyway, what's this about you being back home?"

"Yeah." Claire glances up at me. "I—uh—I got that scholarship I was trying for, remember? They went ahead and awarded it to me effective immediately, so I borrowed Beth's car and drove home."

"Wait, what? You drove two thousand miles, *by yourself?*"

"Um, about that, I wasn't exactly alone..."

Her dad sighs loudly. "Did Griffin have something to do with this?"

"Dad, actually..."

"I'm telling you, Claire, that boy, he rubs me the wrong way. You're an adult and you're going to do what you want, but so help me God, if he derails your college plans..."

I like this guy.

"Dad—" she interrupts. "It's not that. Griffin is..." Claire drags her bottom lip into her mouth and tugs on it before saying, "He's dead."

"What?" is all he manages.

Claire nods although he can't see that. "A lot has happened since you left."

Shuffling sounds in the background. "Griffin is *dead?* Dead? That's it. I'm done. I'm calling it quits. I'm coming back there. I should have never left."

She interrupts him again. "Dad, I'm fine. I promise you, I am. I have an apartment. It's really nice, safe."

"An apartment? How are you affording that? And hold on, you said you didn't come alone?"

Her eyes dart to me again. "Yes, I met someone, Dad. I brought him with me. He's nothing like Griffin, I swear it. Even Rosie approves."

"Rose met him?" Somehow, this seems to settle his nerves.

"Numerous times."

He lets out a breath. "I don't like this, Claire. I feel like I've abandoned you, that I'm failing you as a father by not being there. I mean Christ, your boyfriend, sorry, *ex*-boyfriend, he's dead? Did I hear that right?"

"He was drunk and fell down the stairs. He was in ICU for a while and ended up having *complications*." She puts an extra emphasis on that last word.

"Jesus, Claire. I'm sorry I wasn't there for you. Are you...are you okay? I mean, as okay as you could be?"

I wish there was some way to reassure this man I've never met that I would do anything for his daughter. That the safest place she could possibly be is by my side, because I would quite literally stop at nothing to protect her.

"I am. Really."

And somehow, despite it being a terrible thing to admit, I

think Griffin dying was actually a good thing. He was a menace to everyone he came in contact with. He didn't deserve the air he was breathing. This world will be a better place without him.

"I can come back, Claire."

"No, Dad. I don't want you to. I mean, I do miss you, that's a given. But you're more useful there. Finish out your assignment and write the best damn piece you can. I want this for you, more than I want you here. Do it for me, okay?"

"If you change your mind, I swear it, I'll be on the next flight home." He pauses and adds. "This doesn't feel right. I should be there with you."

"Dad, there isn't anything for you to do. I'm in school full time. I'm working on getting a job. Between that, getting my assignments done, and my social life, there isn't space for much else. I'm telling you, stay there. If I need you, I pinky promise I'll reach out."

"And this guy, you're sure about him?"

She sighs and stares straight at me. "Absolutely."

And with that, the phone disconnects, his prepaid minutes ending abruptly.

"Well, that went well." Claire drops her butt onto the bed and covers her face.

"Could have probably gone worse, considering." I throw my arm around her shoulder. "He cares, though. You have that. Complete polar opposite of your mom. One great parent is better than two shitty ones."

She sighs and leans into me. "Yeah." Claire angles her head to look up at me. "Did you ever meet your dad?"

I avert my gaze, shifting it to the floor. "No." Childhood memories trickle in, none of them very pleasant. My mom, always with some douche who treated her like shit. "I don't think so."

"What if you could, would you?" She stares at me with such curiosity.

I've pondered this same question many times before. The answer always the same. Whoever that man was, he left us. He left her. And maybe her death was her own fault, for going down the wrong path time and time again, but it's hard not to hold someone at least a little accountable for something like that. She never told me anything about him, and at a certain point, I stopped asking. If he could leave her the way he did, he was never someone I wanted to get to know.

"No."

My response seems to surprise her. "Oh."

"Would you?" I ask her.

She shrugs and straightens up. "Maybe. I mean, I'm not you, and you have your own experience. But for me, I'm sort of glad I went out West to be with my mom. It sucked, don't get me wrong, it was a terrible time." She sort of humorlessly laughs. "I wouldn't have met you if I didn't, though. And I wouldn't have known for sure what kind of person she was. I didn't like the not knowing, the wondering if I had it all wrong, and she was actually a decent human. Now, well, now I can make my own judgments without guessing. That woman sucks. Maybe she's a good friend, or a loyal worker, but as a mother, she's the worst."

She has a point. The uncertainty that lingers is a fickle bitch. But there are endless possibilities and I'm not sure if I could handle the truth. And even then, I would have no fucking clue how to go about locating him, if he's even alive. I legit have not a single identifying detail about him. I don't know his name, where he's from, what he looks like—nothing. Only that he knocked my mom up and didn't stick around.

He could be dead. Or he could be a deadbeat. But what if he's actually decent? What if he's an investment banker or a freaking doctor? What if he has other children…a family? I could potentially have brothers or sisters.

I'll never know, though, because not only will it be like finding a needle in a haystack, but I may also not live long enough to start the search. At this rate, Franklin will be coming for me any time now, and I need to focus on preparing for his arrival.

I kiss Claire's cheek. "You have the morning off from class, right?"

Her lips turn up into a smile, a devious grin forming. "Yeah, you thinking what I'm thinking?"

For once, sex is not on my brain. I grab her hand and pull her up from the bed.

Claire's smile immediately turns into a frown. "Ah, come on!"

"Let's get breakfast. We'll have time for that later." I wink at her and weave my fingers around hers.

I would absolutely love to do nothing more than lay in bed with her, rolling around the sheets until it's time for her to go to class, but if I'm going to get on top of the developing deadly situation, I need to do some reconnaissance.

"Are we driving or walking?" Claire slips from my grasp and walks over to her backpack that's resting on the couch in our living room.

"In this weather?" I snort. "Driving."

"I keep forgetting how much you hate the cold." She smiles at me and pulls a book from her bag. "I have to finish a chapter before class."

"It's not the temperature, it's all that wet nasty stuff on the ground out there."

Claire strolls over with a sultry gaze. She leans in close, whispering into my ear. "I could show you something wet and nasty."

Heat flushes over me. How is it possible she takes my dislike for the snow and turns it into something so fucking sexy? If I didn't want to extend the length of my life to give myself more time with her, I'd jump her bones right this instant. The throbbing in my pants is going to have to cool down until we get back.

I might not have long right now, but I steal a kiss from her anyway. I melt my lips onto hers and bring my hand up to grip the side of her face. I dance my tongue into her mouth, delicately caressing it against hers.

Her body reacts immediately, pushing into mine and silently begging me for more.

Instead, I break away, smiling and telling her, "You're out of control."

She grins back. "You made me this way."

The drive across town is quick, and I savor every second of Claire being beside me, my palm stretched out on her thigh as she reads from her book.

I pull into an open parking spot and put the car in park. I patiently wait for her to finish up the last page, watching her ocean blue eyes skim the words in such a captivating manner.

Every single thing she does drives me wild with love and lust and admiration.

I hop out, rushing around to open her door before she gets the chance to. I extend my hand for her to take, and guide her onto the sidewalk.

She stops dead in her tracks and stares up at the building we're in front of.

I slide my fingers around hers and pull her toward the door. It clangs shut behind us, just like the one at Bram's had done.

A place I miss dearly. A place I hope to return to someday.

Bram was the father I never had, and I hate how I took for granted our time together. I had pushed him away when shit got rough, but somehow, he came through for me in ways I never could have expected. I owe him my life for helping me try to escape Franklin, even when he had no idea what was going on.

Claire clings to my arm, and I welcome her closeness.

I point to a booth in the corner. "How about there?"

She nods slightly, a sense of nervousness about her bubbling to the surface. Is it because she can feel my unease, too?

I slide into the seat opposite of Claire, giving myself a solid vantage point with the most optimal viewing of the diner.

A freckle-faced boy with a beanie approaches. He lays two napkins on the table and pulls out a notepad. "What can I get you to drink?"

I glance at Claire but she's fumbling with her thumb.

"Two black coffees. No cream or sugar, just a shaker of cinnamon, please."

The kid eyes me curiously, glances at Claire, and then walks away without another word.

I reach across, grabbing Claire's hand in mine, hoping it will calm whatever nerves she's experiencing. I scan the place, searching for any sign of something out of the ordinary.

The building has a strange resemblance to Bram's. A very old-fashioned diner kind of vibe. Same glass case with various sweets—some muffins, a few pies.

"Is this where you brought that donut home from?" I ask Claire.

She looks up at me, a wildness in her eyes. "Mmhm."

I narrow my gaze. "What's up with you?"

But before she can answer, the kid is back with two mugs and a pot of coffee. He sets down the cinnamon and slides it toward me. "What else can I get you?"

I shift my eyes to the menus near the packets of sugar, but decide to order our usual, in hopes that it's edible. "Two stacks of blueberry pancakes and two orders of bacon. That'll be it for now."

The kid makes a note on his paper. "Shouldn't take long."

He leaves me and Claire behind, our hands still gripping each other.

I sprinkle some cinnamon into her cup and nudge it toward her, doing the same with mine, and then scan the crowd again.

Old couple in the opposite corner booth. A middle-aged woman on her laptop at a table. A twenty-something guy standing near the register, waiting to pay his bill. Another guy kneeling by the donuts trying to figure out which one he wants.

There's the kid serving us, and another young lady wiping down a newly empty table. At least one person working in the kitchen, but from here, I can't pinpoint for sure.

I release Claire and drag my cup to my lips, blowing gently on the steam rising to assault me. I take a sip, noting the decent flavor. Not too bitter but packs a solid bold punch. I will definitely be adding it to my list of coffee shops. Is that why Josey chooses to come here daily? I didn't peg him for a java snob, but maybe he enjoys the laid-back atmosphere and the fact that it's so fucking similar to Bram's. A reminder of back home.

A man appears from the kitchen area, his back pushing through the swinging door, a case of something in his arms. He turns, setting it on the counter and skimming the patrons. His harsh gaze settles over us briefly, but he does a double-take, staying on us longer than the rest of the diner. He glances over to the kid then points and mumbles something about the contents of the box, grabs a pot of coffee off the nearest burner, and walks over.

Claire's body goes rigid the way one would if one saw a ghost.

"Top you off?" He meets my gaze and doesn't look away.

I scan the shape of his face, the dark green shade of his eyes. The way his jaw is pressed in a tense manner. There's something so familiar about him that it's unnerving.

"Sure," I finally respond, pushing my cup toward him and dragging Claire's along, too.

"You take yours with cinnamon, too?" He fills us up and stands there, waiting for my response.

"Mmhm." I glance over to Claire in my peripheral, ready to throw myself across the table if this guy ends up somehow being a threat to her.

"Thought I was the only one." His lips turn up slowly, a strange kindness about the expression on his face. He glances at Claire. "Glad to see you back, Claire."

I fully focus on her again. Have these two already met?

"You and Rosie make friends everywhere, don't you?" I ask Claire a bit rhetorically.

The man raises a bushy eyebrow at her.

Claire forces a smile.

"They sure do. Rosie was a chatty one." He extends his free hand to me. "Luciano Bane."

My attention shifts to the branding on the menu, plastered on the front window...the name of the place. *Bane's Café*. It's no wonder he met Claire and Rosie last night, he's the freaking Bram of this establishment.

I grab hold and give him a firm shake. I catch the wrong word just as it's about to escape my lips and switch it with my hidden identity. "Theo."

"My pleasure." Luciano looks to Claire then to me. "If you need anything, let me know." He strolls away, going back behind the bar and setting the pot of joe on its warmer.

Our young waiter passes him on the way over, hands full of plates of pancakes and bacon.

I scan the room again, not really noticing anything out of place. Maybe I can meet Josey and see if he can help me figure out how to get out of this mess I'm in.

Claire takes a bite of her pancakes, mumbling about how good they are.

I focus on her, smiling at how happy she is with her breakfast. Good food and coffee are the way to my girl's heart, and it's one of the things I absolutely adore about her.

I notice the way her gaze darts across the room toward the kitchen, like she's watching out for something suspicious, too. Is it because of our already sketchy situation, or is there something else causing her to be extra concerned with keeping an eye out?

CLAIRE – 14

*J*ohnny shook his biological father's hand.
 And neither one of them had a fucking clue who the other was.

Johnny probably assumes Luciano is just a random café owner, and Luciano thinks we're only another set of patrons who enjoy his place's food.

I should have paid more attention to where Johnny was taking us, but I really needed to get that chapter read before class, and I had no idea he would bring us to the one place on the entire Eastern Seaboard that we should avoid.

Last night, when I saw Luciano for the first time, I thought there was a strong resemblance, but seeing them together, practically side by side, it was startling how much they resemble each other. Their eyes especially—they're almost the exact same shade of emerald, which in itself is incredibly rare.

I wonder if they noticed it, the similarities between them? Or if they thought it was a weird coincidence that they happened to share a few physical qualities.

One thing that definitely drew my attention was Luciano's quick covering up when Johnny called me out on having Rosie with me. Luciano easily could have thrown me under the bus, but instead, he went right along with it, even layering a strangely believable detail about Rosie being chatty.

Luckily for me, that's how Rosie really is, which made Johnny buy into it even more.

Another lie added onto the stacks of deceit between us. If I don't come clean soon, it's going to raise too much suspicion and create issues with me and Johnny. We've been through too much; I can't afford for us to fight over shit that we can easily handle.

How do I tell him that I fibbed and got his DNA, not to test his allergies, but to see if he had any living relatives, and on top of that, that the man he met earlier for breakfast was his bio dad who I semi-stalked?

Oh, and that I'm pretty sure *I'm* the reason Griffin is dead.

You know, no big deal.

And on top of all of that, it feels like Johnny is hiding something from me, too.

He's been paranoid since the moment we initiated our plan in the hospital, but lately, he's taken it to a whole new level. Constantly looking over his shoulder, quite literally, scanning every single body that passes us, like he's waiting for a threat to form out of thin air.

I don't want to pry too much, because I don't want to draw attention to his paranoia if that's all it really is, but what if there's something he hasn't told me? A danger I'm unaware of. If there is, I should probably stop wandering off on my own, but if there isn't, I don't see any issue with doing a little more investigation into this Luciano Bane, and seeing whether or not he's worthy of being in Johnny's life.

"J..." I place my hand on Johnny's shoulder, pulling his attention from the notepad he's jotting down stuff on.

"What's up?" He immediately pushes it aside and gives me

his full focus. He raises his arm to run his fingers through his hair but stops himself, realizing that his long locks are no more.

"Is everything okay?" I hate the idea that he might be holding back from me, but aren't I doing the same exact thing?

Johnny's brows scrunch together. "Yeah." His expression darkens. "Did something happen?"

I can sense the immediate shift in his heart rate. "No." I take his hands in mine. "I'm just checking on you. Making sure nothing had changed that I should know about."

Johnny sighs, and for a second, I think he's about to confess something to me.

Instead, he shakes his head. "No, nothing you should know about." Johnny brings my knuckles to his mouth and presses soft kisses along them.

Despite it feeling like that's not the whole truth, I don't push anymore. If it were a real concern, he would tell me. It would be foolish of him not to.

"Okay." I tilt his head up to stare into his beautiful eyes. "Good."

I guess that means I'm in the clear to do a bit of digging on Luciano before I decide when or if I'm going to tell Johnny the truth about his father.

J finish class and send Johnny a quick text.

Me: Going to grab coffee again and study a little, want me to bring home dinner?

Johnny: Sure, surprise me. Be safe, okay?

Me: Always. Love you.

Johnny: Love you, more.

"Hey." I pause before Rosie goes her separate way to her car. "You want to go over that Lit material?"

She shrugs and yawns. "If there's some caffeine involved, I'm game."

I smile. "Hop in." I open up the door for her to climb aboard.

I grip the steering wheel firmly on our quick drive to the place I've been twice in the last twenty-four hours. Now about to be a third time. It's strange how I'd never been there in the entire time I lived here, and now I'm frequenting it multiple times in one day. I pull up and put the car into park, hesitating before cutting the engine.

"Wait, is this..." Rosie does a double-take on me and the building we're stopped in front of.

"Yep."

"Holy shit." She relaxes into her seat, allowing me to make the final decision on when we're going to get out. "I can't believe they shook hands."

"Right? It was unnerving. Like watching someone meet themselves from the future."

Rosie squints to peer inside. "You think he's in there?"

I sigh. "It's possible."

"Good, I want to see him."

I reach into the backseat and pull my bag out. If I'm going to be here, I'd prefer to look like I really am studying and not as a total creep. At least this time I'm not alone.

I draw in a breath and grab the door handle, steadying myself for whatever is about to come next. Maybe what I heard last night was a total fluke, and Luciano is simply a café owner and nothing more.

Or there is the very real possibility that he's the equivalent of Franklin—a no-good criminal piece of shit that deserves to rot in hell.

Here's to hoping it's the former. For Johnny's sake.

Rosie and I walk side by side until we reach the entrance. I hold the door open for her and let her go ahead of me.

She goes straight in, claiming the same empty booth Johnny

and I occupied earlier today.

A deep voice sounds from behind me. "We really have to stop meeting like this."

I turn to see Luciano standing right there, a white towel draped over his shoulder, the same way Bram had done many times before.

I swallow down the immediate nerves that rise and force myself to act somewhat fucking normal. "I blame the coffee. It's really good."

Really, Claire? That's what you decide to say?

Luciano stifles a grin, the same way Johnny does. "What can I say, I've spent a lot of time researching and refining which beans we source. I'm glad you appreciate the effort."

Rosie clears her throat.

Luciano extends his hand. "You must be Rosie."

To my surprise, she blushes, but takes his outreaching palm into hers. "I am."

Leave it to Rosie to have the hots for my man's father. I'd kick her in the shin if it wouldn't bring unwanted attention my way.

"Well, ladies, what can I get for you? Coffee?" Luciano raises an eyebrow at me.

"And a lot of cream and sugar." Rosie plops herself into her seat.

"Two cups? Or is your man joining you?"

"Just us," I tell him.

He nods and disappears behind the counter to fetch our drinks.

Rosie's eyes go wide, and she lowers herself toward me. "Oh, my, God," she whisper-shouts. "He's *gorgeous*."

I tilt my head at her. "Seriously?" I flit my gaze in Luciano's direction then back at her. "Cut it out. You're like half his age, and it's J's freaking *dad*." I make sure to be extra quiet on that last part.

"Oh hush, I'm not going to do anything about it." Rosie folds her arms. "You were right though. It's a bit eerie."

I lean against my seat. "Right?"

A waitress brings our cups over and fills them, leaving and returning a moment later with Rosie's cream. "Are you ready to order?"

I shake my head. "I'm good with coffee." I promised Johnny I'd bring home dinner.

"Me too," Rosie adds.

I run my hands through my hair, scratching my scalp and tossing the long brown locks aside. "This is insane."

"Yeah, it really is."

I bring the cup to my lips, savoring the full, untainted flavor of the roast. Bold, a bit smoky, with a hint of something rich, maybe chocolate. It's damn good, to say the very least.

Rosie pours entirely too much cream into her mug and showers it with an ungodly amount of sugar. "What are you going to do?"

I only now remember that I forgot to ask for cinnamon. I take another drink anyway. "I'll be right back." Before I can overthink it, I slither out of the booth and through the front door without drawing the attention of anyone other than Rosie.

Once outside, I cautiously glance around and then sneak into that same alley as last night. I tiptoe quietly along the side of the building, careful not to make a sound. A bright light shines from the back, a few muted voices floating around. I strain to make them out to no success. I get a little closer, and then a little more.

I inch further and further until there's barely any shadow left to hide in. My heart races but more with exhilaration than fear. I shouldn't be here; I shouldn't be so foolish, but I have to find out more about this mystery man. I don't want to keep this secret from Johnny any longer than I have to, and I refuse to come forward without more information.

I press my side into the brick and brace myself with my hand to lean a bit more.

"Twelve shipments, East End," one of the people says.

"Should have been fifteen," the other corrects.

A long sigh. Some shuffling. The sound of a door closing, then silence.

I hold my breath, waiting for the voices to return. For something other than the very generic bits and pieces I've already heard. It's not enough to go on. Those deliveries could have easily been related to the café, not an illicit activity.

I blink and in a flash, my body is flipped against the wall, a hand wrapped around my throat, pressing tightly and pinning me in place.

Attached to it is the man in question, towering over me with a fierce glare. "Who are you working for?"

My mouth drops open, but words don't come out. I'm too stunned by the intensity of the situation. Still, this doesn't confirm whether or not he's involved with something illegal. Maybe he's just an incredibly protective coffee shop owner.

He tightens his grip. "Don't make me ask again, who are you and Theo working for?"

I narrow my gaze at him and attempt to shake my head. "No one." I clench my own hands around his forearm to try to pry him away.

"I don't believe you." Luciano clenches his jaw. "Out of nowhere, you two show up at my place four times, poking your noses around where you shouldn't be."

Four? I've only been here three, unless…unless Johnny came here without me?

But why would he have done that? He was acting rather curious when we were here this morning. Did it have something to do with that? Does Johnny somehow already know the truth about the owner of the café? How would that even be possible? I have only looked at the results once, and that was on campus, when Johnny wasn't around. If it's not that, maybe Johnny knows something I don't, that Luciano really is involved with a part of Johnny's past that he's trying to put behind him.

"I…" What am I supposed to tell him? The truth? That I'm lurking in the shadows because he's my boyfriend's father, and I'm trying to determine his worth prior to telling Johnny? But if I do, that opens up a whole new can of worms. And I'd rather Johnny know the truth before this random dude with his hand gripping my throat.

But if I don't tell him, he's going to suspect I'm working against him, and maybe he'll use the same professional courtesy Franklin has done to people who messed with him, and end my life for the sheer fact that he can.

Luciano's nostrils flare as he lets out a breath. "Tell me who."

I frantically stare back and forth between his green eyes. They're so fucking similar to Johnny's.

"I am not a man you want to cross, Claire…if that's even your name." Luciano looks toward the street when a few people walk by, but we're tucked into the shadows no one would be able to see us without venturing down this dark path. "Are you here on behalf of Franklin?"

With that name, I practically see red. The person who nearly took Johnny from me. The man that I desperately hope gets what's coming to him.

Luciano cocks his head slightly. "You're not, are you?"

I slowly rock my head from side to side. "No."

Something seems to click within him, and his resolve softens. He doesn't let me go, but his grip loosens barely. "Why are you here?"

"The coffee," I spit out.

Luciano narrows his gaze once more. "I'm losing my patience with you." His fingers twitch around my neck, like he's about to squeeze it again and force the answer out of me.

I let my mind wander, to the very real possibility that Johnny finds out what happens tonight, and the reaction he'll have once he finds out what his father did. I cannot allow Luciano to leave a mark of what he did, because Johnny may never forgive him. Luciano isn't exactly winning any father of the year awards, but I'd be setting him up for immediate failure if he hurt a hair on my head.

The only thing I can do is tell him the truth, even if he doesn't believe me.

"Theo is your son."

Luciano stares at me, not saying a thing.

Is he in shock?

His lips part and his eyes wander then meet mine again. "That's not...possible."

"Lynne," I say.

"No." Luciano's hand falls from me, dropping to his side.

I bring my own up to my neck in an automatic response to being held so aggressively. I study him while an unrecognizable flurry of emotions rushes over him.

He rakes his fingers through his hair, another thing Johnny has a habit of doing. A second passes in uncomfortable silence before he looks at me again, a pang of sadness in his eyes. "I'm so sorry."

And somehow, I truly believe it. If he really is in the dark world I think he is, it's no shock that he reacted the way he did. I probably would have done the same if I were in his shoes. It's difficult to know who to trust when everyone is against you.

"You can't tell him," I blurt out.

"He doesn't know?" Luciano's brows bunch together in disbelief.

I rub my neck. "No, not yet...I..."

He tugs at his bunched-up sleeve, pulling it down. "How? How did you find out?"

I bite at my lip, hating to recall another one of my deceitful moments. "An ancestry thing."

"Why?" Luciano's stare is serious and intense.

"Joh—," I stop myself too late and hope he didn't catch that slip. "Theo doesn't have anyone else. It's just me. I don't want that for him. Heaven forbid, if something happened to me—he'd be alone. He doesn't deserve that."

Luciano stands there, shock rattling his features. He lets out a breath. "I'm…speechless."

I want to ask him questions, figure out why he left Lynne and Johnny, but this isn't exactly the time or place. Rosie will start to wonder where I've been, and I can't keep Johnny waiting much longer. He already worries enough; I don't want to make that worse.

"I have to go." I point my thumb toward the street.

That seems to snap Luciano out of his trance. "Sure, yeah." He holds his hand out between us, signaling me to wait. "Listen, I really am sorry." He motions to his neck. "I…" Luciano shakes his head. "I shouldn't have done that."

"Water under the bridge." Because if I don't put it in the past, and Johnny finds out, there will be hell to pay. And I don't blame him; I would do the same. I turn to walk away but stop myself, something he had said earlier nagging at my thoughts. "You mentioned four times that we had been in. I've only been in three."

Luciano averts his gaze slightly before returning to me. "My mistake. I'm probably just paranoid."

But I'm not stupid, and Luciano is in the type of business where you can't make those types of errors. He had covered up for me with Johnny about the Rosie thing, and now he's doing the same for Johnny.

Why would Johnny come to the diner without telling me? What is he hiding?

I know damn well it's not another woman, so it has to be something that involves the past we're trying to escape. That would be the only reason Johnny would keep a secret from me.

JOHNNY – 15

One of my favorite parts of living with Claire is watching her get ready in the morning.

From that first moment of opening her sleepy eyes, it's like I fall in love again every single day. Each time deeper than the last. My heart never really sure how it's possible to feel the way I do about another person, but allowing it to happen without reservation.

Sure, the possibility of her leaving me fucking wrecks me to consider, but I cherish the moments I have with her, just in case it's my last. One day, Claire might realize she's too good for me, and decide she's had enough of hiding in the shadows and living a half-life. She deserves more than this constantly looking over your shoulder existence that I've drug her into.

Claire pauses, her hand on her jutted-out hip. Her black lace panties hug her in such a way it makes the blood rush straight to my dick.

"This is where I tell you to take a picture, so it'll last longer." Claire grins at me and steps closer to the edge of the bed.

"And I'd respond with something stupid, I'm sure, like…can

I?" I reach up, grabbing her by the hands and tugging her on top of me.

Claire giggles but doesn't protest, climbing up and straddling my waist. "We don't have time." But instead of hopping off of me, she leans down and presses her lips to mine, our bodies coming alive in a flash.

"Then we'll be quick," I breathe into her between kisses. I wrap my arm around her and flip her onto her back. I break away from her mouth and make a trail straight down her neck, her stomach, and hover around her panty line. I tug them to the side, swirling my tongue confidently in all the places I know drive her wild.

She arches her body toward me, telling me that I'm doing exactly what she needs.

I slide a finger in place, rocking it gently while my mouth does most of the work. Sucking and licking and appreciating her like the goddess she is. I feel her tension build, my own pleasure rising with hers. I reach up with my free hand, twisting and teasing her nipple gently.

Claire's attention shifts as she fumbles with the stack of condoms sitting on our bedside table. She rips one open and drags me up, her lips cascading onto mine while she tugs down my boxers and secures the thing over my ready cock.

I'm careful sliding into her, partially because entering her might just be my favorite thing ever.

She lets out a moan in response and pivots herself toward me. Her hands grip my back, inching me into her even more.

I lift her with one arm, the other propping me up. I thrust gently in and out, deeper and deeper, and when I sense her climax, I let mine ride along with hers in tandem.

"Johnny," she whispers. Claire's mouth meets mine in a chaos of lust and passion and desire that could never be satiated. An intense love that is impossible to replicate.

With one final plunge, we come crashing down together, maintaining a slow and steady pace to lengthen the pleasure.

It's everything all at once, the most extreme high I could ever imagine.

Every single time, I think it can't possibly get any better, yet somehow it does. The more we're with each other, the stronger our connection becomes, the more powerful the experience.

Claire grins and brings her plush lips to mine once again. "I really have to go."

And although I'd love nothing more than to keep her here with me, tucked safely away from any kind of harm that could come her way, I sigh and hop off the bed, letting her escape me.

I have work that needs to be done anyway—strategizing with Josey in an attempt to figure out how to evade Franklin for good. I had met with Josey yesterday, but it was cut short when his pressing family situation called him out. We only had a few minutes in that Bram's lookalike diner before he had to go. I'm hopeful that today will give us a bit more room to come up with something, considering I'm at pretty much ground zero on what I'm going to do.

Claire finishes getting ready and stands by the front door, waiting for our almost ritualistic goodbye: a hug that never seems to last long enough, and a kiss that puts those Hollywood romances to shame. We both hate being away from each other, that's for damn sure. But she needs to get her education, and I have to work on preserving our lives.

After killing a couple hours once she's gone, I slip out of the security of our apartment and onto the street. I could easily take an Uber across town, but I use the time to get a little more acquainted with my surroundings, just in case. Plus, I hear the exercise helps in the recovery process, and I'd like to do what I can to get back to one hundred percent.

I definitely don't recommend getting shot, especially the way that I did. Most people would have spent a few extra days in the hospital, stayed on bed rest, and recovered normally. Me? I planned an elaborate fake death and spent close to three days in the backseat of a car, stopping occasionally for medical care and constantly worrying that my attacker would be hot on our tail. It wasn't ideal, but we did what we had to do, given the circumstances.

I'm pretty much fine now, just a bit achy here and there. Something that probably wouldn't be an issue if there wasn't a psychopath wanting to finish me off.

The air is crisp and cold. I hug my arms around me and continue along the main road, coming up on Claire's university. The invisible thread tethering us together tightens with her near proximity. There's a strong pull to wander toward it, just to see her, to confirm that she's safe and sound, but I ignore it and keep on my way. There's no real reason she should be in any immediate danger—not yet.

I glance at my watch, noting the time and how long it took me to get here. The walk wasn't as bad as I expected, not with the snow being mostly gone. I grip the metal handle of the door, the little bells heralding my entry when I pull the door open. I stroll in like I own the place and go straight to the booth in the corner. The one with the best view.

Two older women sit at a small table, sipping their tea. A guy close to my age, with thick-rimmed glasses, is nose-deep in a book a few feet away from the ladies. The kid with the beanie is working again, wiping down a table.

He glances over at me and tips his head up to acknowledge me. "I'll be right there."

I repeat the gesture. "You're fine."

The door to the kitchen swings open and Luciano appears. His eyes widen when he sees me.

What the hell has gotten into him?

Luciano grabs a cup and a pot of coffee and comes over. He

pours it without saying anything, his hand almost shaking a little.

"Thanks." The word sort of comes out of my mouth like a question.

"Mmhm," he mumbles. "Can I get you anything else?"

The beanie kid comes over. "I can take over from here, boss."

Luciano shoos him away. "I've got it, Miller."

Miller side-eyes him but shrugs and walks away, probably grateful for the reprieve from working. For such a young fellow, he sure does seem worn out. The bags under his eyes are dark and heavy.

"No, I'm fine," I answer Luciano's question. "I'm just waiting for someone."

Luciano bobs his head up and down. "I see. Claire joining you?"

At just the sound of her name leaving his lips, a fire ignites within me, the possessiveness of keeping her safe overpowering the very normalness of the inquiry.

I relax my clenched jaw. "No. A friend."

Luciano's eyes dart to the seat across from me and then back to me, like he's nervous about something. This is not how he acted the night I met him with Claire. Then, he seemed confident and cocky, arrogant even. Now he's being…weird.

"Are you all right?" I'm not really sure why I ask this.

"Yes. I—um."

The bell dings, alerting us to another patron in the diner.

Josey strolls over, slapping Luciano on the back like they're longtime pals. "Lucy." He slides into the unoccupied seat and points to the pot still in Luciano's hand. "I'll have a cup."

Luciano blinks at him, then at me, then at him again. "You two know each other?"

"Ah, yeah, we go way back." Josey points his big-ass arm at me.

I watch as the wrong name forms on his lips, but he immediately catches it.

"Theo just moved to town. I was going to show him around."

Luciano meets my gaze again. "Is that right?"

I nod. "Yep."

Why does he act like he's doubting what we're saying? Who does this guy think he is? And why does it matter either way? Who is he to Josey?

Luciano lets it go, focusing on Josey. "I'll get you a mug." He turns toward Miller. "Another coffee over here."

"Yes, sir," Miller replies obediently, going straight over and fetching a cup.

I stare at Josey. "What was that all about?"

"What?" He stirs some sugar into his java, completely oblivious. Finally, he meets my gaze. "Lucy? That was nothing. He's just nosy. Don't worry about him."

I glance toward the kitchen, catching Luciano peeking out from behind the open window area. He moves quickly to avoid eye contact. That was definitely not nothing. The dude is creeping me out.

"I mean, don't cross him, that's for sure. But you're a new face. He's letting his need to know everything get the best of him." Josey tilts his cup to his lips, taking a hearty swig even though steam is pouring from the piping hot brew. "Honestly, this is the safest place for us to meet. You don't have to worry about anything shady here." He nonchalantly sets his drink down and throws his arm over the back of his seat. "So, you wanted to talk to me."

But with the sudden weight of Luciano's mysterious stare, I no longer think that involving Josey is the best idea. Maybe I should stick with my gut and handle all of this on my own. Without his help, though, I'm up shit creek without a paddle. I don't know which direction I'd row even if given the opportunity.

Ever since Claire walked into my life, I haven't had to do any of this alone. Even when I tried to keep her out of it, she managed to barge in and take control of each situation, navigating me through the thick of it. I wouldn't have made it this far without her, and I'm a fool for thinking I'll get through the rest of it. She helped me find that package, plan the entire faking my death scheme, and has managed to nurse me back to health. Shit, she brought up all of my grades, maintained hers, and scored a competitive scholarship, all while navigating a criminal underground.

We're a team, and we've made that known. That's not going to change. Why am I struggling so damn much to involve her?

Because I don't want her to get hurt. That's why.

There have been too many close calls. Too many moments when Claire could have been seriously injured. With Griffin. With Jared. With all of this. What if that shooter missed on her birthday and shot her instead of me? The idea of Claire being caught in the crossfire is enough to make me want to wrap her up in a bubble and never let her go.

"You've got this wild look on your face, JJ." Josey takes another drink.

"There's got to be something I can do to stop him, right?"

Josey rakes his hand across his jaw. "I mean, other than putting a bullet between his eyes?" He glances around the diner and then back to me. "You really pissed him off."

If only he'd tell me something I don't already know.

"Why does he care so much? Doesn't he have better shit to deal with than chasing me down?" It's petty, even for a mob boss.

"Principle. If word gets around that he knew what you did and he let it slide, people will think he went soft." Josey lets out a breath. "This *business* is ruthless, you've seen it."

One too many times. I shake the thoughts out of my head,

not wanting to relive the things I've witnessed Franklin have his men carry out.

That sick glint of power that Franklin always had. He enjoys his job more than he should.

"What about..." I lower my voice and lean forward. "The feds?"

Josey laughs. "You think people haven't tried? The dude's hands are clean. That's what he has grunts like us for."

He's right. Franklin was sure to be careful about that kind of thing. Making us do his bitch work. But he's only human. He could have slipped up at least once.

My phone buzzes in my pocket, and I drag it out to see Claire's face across the screen. I press my finger to my lips to signal Josey to not say a word. I hit the green button and accept the call.

"Babe, what's going on?"

Claire sniffles. "I didn't want to call you, I tried to fix it myself. I'm sorry."

My heart picks up its pace, a million different situations run through my head. "Claire, where are you? What happened? I'm coming right now." I hop up from the booth, digging my hand into my pocket. I throw a five-dollar bill onto the table and make my way to the door, completely ignoring everyone in the place.

"I'm in front of the parking garage." Claire exhales. "I got a flat tire."

And like I can finally fucking breathe again, I clutch my hand to my chest. "Oh, sweetheart. It's okay. Shit happens."

Of all the things I had thought of, this was definitely at the back of the list. This outcome being the best worst-case scenario.

"Hop in the car and wait for me. I'll be right there."

"Okay," she says with such defeat in her tone.

"Everything is fine. Don't worry. I'll be there soon. I love you."

"I love you."

We hang up and I turn around to see Josey coming after me.

"Car trouble, dude. I've got to go."

"You need a hand?" He points in the direction I was heading.

"Not a chance. She still doesn't know you're in town."

Josey widens his eyes and nods his head. "Ah. I got it. She's a feisty one, though, I'd be careful keeping secrets from her."

Ain't that the damn truth. I fucking hate that I haven't told her about what's going on. I just want to attempt to have some kind of solution to the problem before I spring it on her. The last thing I want her to be concerned about is how to help me. I should be the one taking care of her, not the other way around.

"I'll catch you later, man." My sights land on Luciano as he pretends to clean off a table; in reality he's eyeing us from his place inside the diner.

There's something seriously off about that guy, and once I figure out how to live a little longer, I'm going to find out what his deal is.

I jog the rest of the way to Claire's location, pleased with my ability to not completely get out of breath despite the lack of exercise since my near-death experience.

Claire jumps out when she sees me. "Why did you come from that direction?" She narrows her gaze at me immediately.

"What?" Fuck. "I was uh—out for a walk, when you called." I tap on the trunk. "Will you pop it so I can grab the spare?"

She reaches down and pulls the latch, but doesn't take her eyes off of me. "Johnny."

I lift up the mat in the back and sigh in relief at the sight of the full-size spare. At least I won't have to track down a tire shop and get a replacement. One less problem despite the many others piling up.

Claire leans her hip on the side of the car and crosses her arms. "Where were you?"

This is my moment to come clean. To tell her about Josey. About Franklin. The note he left in the mailbox of our old apartment. To confess that I'm scared, that I'm completely in over my head and I'm not sure how I'm going to get us out of this mess. To apologize for ever getting her involved in the first place. To drop to my knees and beg her for forgiveness for everything I've put her through since she met me. To stomach the pain of watching her walk away when she realizes there's no coming back from the darkness Franklin has consumed us in.

My mouth opens, ready to say the words I've held in for far too long. Instead, I blurt out, "Can you grab that tool kit?"

"Seriously?" Claire snatches it out of the trunk and tosses it onto the ground next to me.

It clangs loud enough to gather the attention of the two college kids on the opposite side of the street.

"What happened to us being a team?"

Without looking, I can tell there are tears in her eyes—a sixth sense developed from loving someone so fucking intensely.

I focus on the task at hand, walking around her and getting the jack out of the trunk, bringing it around, and positioning it in place.

"You're not even going to say anything?" This time, there's anger in her voice.

It's not at all misplaced. I'd be pissed at me, too.

"Can we talk when we get home?" I don't dare tilt my head up at her, because I know the second I see her face I'll lose every single bit of strength left in me. "Please."

"Whatever." She turns on her heel and takes off, kicking up a trail of wet debris in her wake.

"Claire." I sigh and stand. "Wait."

Somehow, this stops her. "I need a moment away from you."

There's so much hurt written across her delicate features. "I'll be home soon. Right now, I just need some space."

That familiar tether pulls taut, threatening to rip my heart in two. How did I let things get this out of control? To the point that she doesn't want to be around me. All because I wanted to keep her safe.

I run my hand through my stupid short hair, gawking as she disappears around the corner and out of sight.

I will let her go, for now. She's not in any immediate danger with Franklin still in place. She just needs to cool down. Then she'll come back to me, and I'll tell her anything she wants to know. I refuse to allow anything else to break us apart.

CLAIRE – 16

When did Johnny and I decide to keep secrets from each other?

What happened to us?

We've been through some of the worst shit anyone could imagine, and here we are, being fools and hiding shit.

If I know Johnny, he's doing what he thinks is protecting me. The same exact thing I'm doing to him. But are we really saving each other from anything if we're putting a wedge between us? At the end of the day, aren't *we* the most important part?

It doesn't make his omissions any less painful to experience. And I imagine if he knew I was withholding something, he'd feel the same.

I round the corner, already my emotions settling with the distance from him. Now, all I can think about is running back to him, wrapping my arms around him, and hugging him tightly. Confessing everything I've been keeping from him, and airing every single piece of dirty laundry.

Why did I think *space* is what we needed? It's to tell the damn truth. To be honest with each other and stop assuming that secrets are what's going to help our relationship.

I glance up, noticing I've mindlessly walked myself over to Bane's Café. Part of me wishes I could teleport to Bram's, sit down at the counter, and have him give me a slice of his world-class wisdom. That isn't possible, though, at least not with the newness of faking Johnny's death. Maybe in the future, I could play pretend as the grieving girlfriend, but I'm not sure I could stomach being in the same vicinity where Johnny was almost taken from me forever.

As much as I love Bram and his diner, it's been tainted red.

Instead, I go inside Bane's and walk to the register. I wipe at my face, hoping I don't appear like a total mess. "Two coffees, to go."

A peace offering of sorts. The ice that will break the tension, which will lead to us working through this weird rough patch.

I reach into my pocket to pull out my phone, where I have my cash and cards attached to the case. Except, I come up empty-handed. I feel around the front and back.

"Fuck," I spit out. I dig my fingers into my tiny front pockets, relief washing over me when I feel a bill tucked inside. I wiggle it out, even more relieved to see it'll at least cover our drinks.

Luciano comes out from the kitchen area. "It's on the house." He nudges Miller aside and pushes a few buttons on the screen.

Miller rolls his eyes but grabs our cups and pours them full.

Grabbing the cinnamon shaker on his way, Luciano strolls over. "Do you have a minute?"

After the biggest fight Johnny and I have ever had? "Not really."

"Those tables need cleaned," Luciano tells Miller.

Basically, in a *give us some privacy* kind of way.

I put a dash of cinnamon in each of the coffees and secure the lids.

Luciano tilts his body toward me, away from the rest of the diner. "I believe you."

I meet his gaze. "Why would I have lied about something like that?"

He lifts his shoulder. "People have done crazier things to weasel their way in and out of my presence."

Who does he think he is? "I didn't know who you were until a few days ago. Don't act all high and mighty."

I probably shouldn't take this tone with him, but my emotions are still running wild given the evening I'm having. All I really want is to go home and tell Johnny how sorry I am for storming away. For being childish and reacting the way I did. He's not the only one keeping secrets. We're both guilty, and if we had to weigh them all out, mine is probably worse. He must be worried sick about me, especially now that I know I left my phone in the car. In any other instance, he could track my location and make sure I'm safe and sound.

With Griffin, he demanded I keep that turned on for him, but in a way to control me, to keep his thumb on me and make sure I wasn't cheating on him. With Johnny, he really does put my wellbeing at the top of his priorities. He didn't even want to turn it on, because of my past with Griffin. I insisted, though, knowing it would ease his nerves about me going back to school full time. I wouldn't be going far, but he'd have the ability to check if something had happened and I was taken off course.

Franklin is such a wild card—we haven't been fully confident we escaped him just yet. Maybe with more time. It's still a little too fresh, though.

"You're right," Luciano admits. He runs his hand along his bearded face and into his hair. "This has been…a shock, to say the least. Something I didn't see coming."

I can tell he wants to talk, to vent about the situation. And if I had more time, I would sit down and hear him out, but I can't allow the gap between me and Johnny to grow any larger.

"It wasn't expected on our end either." I shift my tone to be softer. "But I can't get into it right now. I have to get home. We'll discuss this soon, okay?"

"Yeah?" This seems to calm him.

"Yeah."

He sighs, a twinkle appearing in his emerald eyes. "Okay."

I walk out into the cold, grateful for the warm cups in my hands. Was it this chilly when I came here? Or was I fueled by my emotions to the point I ignored the nip at my skin?

I glance both ways, suddenly realizing that I don't have my phone's GPS to guide me. I'll have to figure this out from memory. I'll follow the signs leading me to campus, and make my way from there. It shouldn't be too difficult to manage, each step getting me closer to the man who is my home.

Commotion from behind me catches my attention, but when I look, the people scatter into an alley. My heart stutters, the very realness of being out here alone, in the dark of night, creeping into me. The measly streetlights only do so much to illuminate my path.

I turn back, stopping abruptly when a man wearing a ski mask is standing directly in front of me. Without thinking, I throw one of the still steaming coffees at him.

He flinches and I shift the other direction, only to find another man there, too.

Panicked, I toss the other one and try to evade him.

Anticipating my attack, he dodges out of the way, hissing insults. He grabs hold of my arms, holding me in place while the first guy puts something over my head, completely concealing my vision.

Fuck.

I kick and scream, but it all happens too fast. My body being picked up, the sound of a van door opening, the thud of them dropping me inside and closing me in, the squealing of the tires. I slam against the side of the cold interior as we whip around a corner.

I reach for the burlap sack on my head, ripping it off in one motion. I blink, blink again. But there's nothing but darkness. The back of this vehicle is pitch fucking black. I desperately try to get my eyes to adjust but I struggle to see even my hands in front of my face.

I grip the metal floor, bracing myself for the turns and accelerated motions.

I breathe deeply in an attempt to calm myself.

Okay, Claire, how are you going to get out of this?

My mind shifts to Johnny, and the continued distance between us.

He has to know something is wrong, right? For once, I pray he doesn't listen and actually give me the space I asked for. But even then, how will he find me? I left my phone in our car, and I didn't exactly tell him where I was going.

I shake my head in the dark. I'm on my own. And if I want to make it out of this, I'm going to have to fight.

I feel around the side until my hands locate the back door. I tug at the handle. Of course, it's locked, what kind of kidnappers would leave it in any other position?

The van slows so I do the only thing that comes to mind.

I play dead. Or well, in this case, passed out.

I lay there, my eyes shut enough that I can still see the darkness through them. My arms limp to my side.

We come to a complete stop, my body shifting forward at the abruptness. The engine cuts. Two doors open, then slam shut. Mumbling ensues.

"You do it," one of them says.

"Whatever, man, you're such a pussy."

"She doesn't even look eighteen, dude. You know how much trouble we can get into if we get caught?"

They approach the tail of the van.

I struggle to keep my breathing shallow and my body still.

"You're worried about *the cops*? Seriously?" The guy chuckles.

"You clearly haven't been in this business long."

The door cracks open, a bit of light peering in.

"See, she's fucking out. This is cake."

One of the guys climbs in after me, I'm not sure which, and I don't really care.

He does exactly what I want, moving right into the trap I've set for him.

The second he's in place, I bring my leg up as hard as I can and kick him straight in his man parts.

"Fucking bitch," he wails, falling against the interior with his hands gripping his privates.

I jump up in a flash, darting out and around the stunned guy still standing at the door.

"Get her, you fucking idiot."

For the smallest fleeting moment, I think I've duped them. But the man I assaulted gathers his bearings and takes off after me.

I break into a sprint, the sound of his footsteps fueling me to run even faster.

But it doesn't matter, I'm no match to the length of his strides or the adrenaline-induced dash from being temporarily taken down by a girl.

Frantically, I glance around, hoping like hell I can find some escape. Darkness all around me. A vast open area. Empty industrial buildings, all of them looking exactly the same. Deserted, empty, promising no way out.

The guy grunts loudly while extending his arm, grabbing the mass of brown hair flowing behind me.

I scream out in pain, but it's no use. No one can hear me. And that's exactly why they brought me here. They knew what they were doing. The one guy may be inexperienced at this kind of thing, but the one with his fist tangled in my hair is at least a bit seasoned enough to take me some place remote. Isolated from people hearing my cries for help.

"Come here, you bitch."

I grit my teeth through the throbbing ache on my skull. I swing my fist, landing the side of it on the guy's throat.

He coughs but doesn't let go. Instead, he grips me tighter, dropping me to my knees with the control he has over me.

"Are you going to help me or just stand there?" He calls out to his accomplice.

I struggle to get a look at him, the dark obstructing my view of his face.

The other guy approaches, binding my hands behind my back, but not as aggressively as I would have suspected the guy holding onto me would have done.

"There, try punching me again." The meaner of the two drags me to my feet, pulling me toward the van we arrived in.

"I can still kick you in the nuts," I say through gritted teeth.

He digs his hand in further, tilting my head toward him. "I'd like to see you fucking try."

It's then that he comes a little into focus. His face is riddled with scars, a large one on his brow and across his cheek. Dark, piercing eyes. A cold, unpalatable expression. Is this what Johnny would have eventually turned into if he never escaped Franklin's grasp?

No, that's impossible. Johnny is too good, too pure of a soul for that to have happened.

The man in front of me is nothing but a pathetic waste of oxygen.

His friend might not be as hostile, but he's just as guilty by aiding him.

I'm dragged into one of the vacant structures and tied to a putty-colored metal chair.

With the pull of a chain, a single bulb illuminates the space around us. I want to roll my eyes at the cliché of it all.

I wiggle in my seat, my stomach sinking at the realization that it's secured to the concrete floor below my feet. The smell of bleach fills my nostrils and only furthers the panic that courses through me.

Someone was killed here. And the mess was cleaned up.

It's very possible that my life will end here, too.

The only thing on my mind is the regret of not making it back to Johnny in time, to tell him the truth, and to come clean about everything between us. Our last memory can't be of us fighting.

The brown-eyed guy hands the other a tablet. "Here, you figure it out."

My sights take in the other man, much younger than his partner, probably close to my age, maybe a little older. He casts a glance at me and focuses on his task. Regret hangs in his blue eyes. He's well aware that what he's doing is fucked up, but he goes along with it anyway, probably knowing he has no other choice.

With a final click of a button, ringing sounds, followed by the connection of a call.

He flips the thing around, and my suspicions are finally confirmed.

"Claire Cooper."

A chill creeps up my spine. I've never actually seen him before, but he's exactly how Johnny had described.

"Franklin," I greet him.

He brings a cigar to his lips, taking a drag and letting the smoke billow from his mouth. Slowly, he places it in a crystal dish and leans back into his chair. He's sitting at a table with white linen, hideous red and black paper lining the wall behind him.

Oh, what I wouldn't give to hop through and wring his neck for what he did to Johnny.

"So, you do know who I am." A wicked grin snakes its way up his face. "Quite the elaborate setup you and Mr. Jones pulled off."

I tighten my jaw but don't say anything.

"Listen, Claire, you and I...we have no qualms. Sure, you helped orchestrate Johnny's escape, but I'm willing to put that aside and spare your life." Franklin drums his fingers on the table. "The things you kids do for *puppy love*." He lets out a grave chuckle.

Is he really insinuating what Johnny and I share is comparable to a juvenile crush?

Brown-eyed guy repositions himself, shifting his weight from one foot to the other.

Franklin continues, "All I want is Johnny. It's that simple."

Finally, I ready myself to speak. "You killed him." It's not entirely a lie. Johnny and I both died a little that day.

"You actually expect me to believe that?" Franklin leans forward. "You think I didn't have my nephew followed?" His tone is condescending, as if I should know what he's talking about.

"Your nephew?"

Franklin laughs dryly. "Josey."

Josey? What does he have to do with anything? Is he here? Is that why Johnny has been so fucking weird lately? Because he's been meeting with Josey? Johnny isn't foolish enough to make such a stupid mistake, is he?

He trusts Josey, and Franklin played right into that. If anyone could squeeze him out, other than me, of course it would be Josey.

"I don't know what you're talking about." Which is the honest to God truth.

Franklin nods at the cruel man standing in front of me.

The guy steps forward, draws his arm back and slams it against my face.

Sharp pain spreads through me, and hot sticky liquid runs down my chin. I jut out my tongue to feel the split in my lip then clench my jaw through the pain. I refuse to show them any weakness.

"Is that all you got?" I shouldn't taunt such a twisted fuck, but I do it anyway. Chances of me living to tell the story are slim to none, might as well make it interesting while it lasts.

"Cocky little spitfire, aren't you?" Franklin points his finger through the screen. "You know, Johnny used to do the same. Take his beatings like a good little boy."

Franklin knew the exact thing to say to get me to react, and I do that very thing.

I yank forward, my arms being held back behind me by the ropes, pulling tighter as I fight to get away. As if somehow getting loose would help me get any closer to the man calling the shots. Only, he's probably thousands of miles away, technology the thing linking us together.

"You're a fucking coward." My insult is thrown at Franklin but applicable to everyone standing in this room.

All for what? Because Johnny refused to let Franklin abuse an innocent child. Because he saw someone in need of help and did everything he could to free said person. How does Franklin not see how fucking sadistic he's being?

Franklin clears his throat and taps at his nose, a signal of sorts.

The evil guy lets out an annoyed sigh and reaches into the waistband of his pants, pulling out a pistol. He slides the chamber, securing a bullet in place and points it directly at me.

My heart stutters. Is this really happening? I'm going to be killed because I didn't cooperate? Why am I surprised? This is the kind of bullshit Franklin does. He plays God, because he can.

"All you have to do is give me an address." Franklin's tone is softer but still harsh. "The rest will be taken care of, and I assure you, you'll never hear from me again."

"I'll pass."

The kid's eyes go wide. His mouth slightly parts like he's in disbelief of my words.

The side of the gun slams into my face, a newfound wave of pain following in its wake. Blood trickles down, and I have to squint to see straight.

"Are you sure, Claire? I'm a reasonable man. I'd understand if you reconsidered."

I stare straight at the screen. "I'd rather die."

"Very well." Franklin seems completely unbothered. "I'll find him with or without you."

I wouldn't put it past him to have wanted to do this for the fun of it. Just to watch someone suffer at his hand. And to twist the figurative knife into Johnny that much more. To show Johnny that he calls the shots, and that he won't be trifled with.

The guy brings the barrel of the gun only inches away from my forehead.

This is it. I'm going to be murdered, my blood cleaned up with a splash of bleach. What will happen to my body? What will my dad think? How will Rosie react? Will Johnny ever forgive me? I'd give anything to turn back time and change the outcome of this situation, at least the part where Johnny's under the impression that I'm mad at him.

Does he know how much I love him? From the moment I met him, our souls were intertwined in a way I'll never fully understand. I'll be forever grateful for our tiny infinity. The feelings I have for him will traverse whatever follows—in this life and the next.

I squeeze my eyes shut and whisper, "I love you, Johnny."

Franklin may control the outcome of what happens here, but he won't take my final words.

I'll be waiting for you, I urge the connection between us to give him this parting message.

The last thing I hear is the sound of a gunshot echoing through the building.

JOHNNY – 17

Something doesn't feel right. Something deep within my gut.

Claire and I never fight. Even with everything we've been through, we've never taken time from each other. Maybe a walk to the other room, but not like this. In the beginning, before we were a couple, we avoided each other like the plague, but there was always the undeniable pull to be near each other. It's what eventually drew us together.

I could just be being paranoid, given everything else going on. But what if I'm not?

She asked me for space, I should give that to her.

I pull my phone from my pocket. If I can just see where she is, that little red dot, and know that she's safe, I'll continue to respect her wishes. I unlock the screen and click over to her contact, impatiently waiting for the circle to zoom in and show me her whereabouts.

It's nearly next to my own dot.

She's home?

I rush to the front door, peering outside for her. My heart pounds wildly, like I'll be seeing her for the first time ever.

Everything in me is aching to be beside her, to drag her into me and tell her how sorry I am. To confess everything.

But she doesn't appear. I glance down at the screen again, frantically hoping her dot gets closer to mine. It doesn't move.

I let the door shut behind me as I make my way toward her. I rush along the hallway, down the stairs and into the large foyer of our building. I take another look at my phone and continue my approach to the red circle. I pop outside, startled to find myself standing in front of the car I bought for Claire.

Was she so upset with me that she's hanging out in there instead of coming upstairs?

I peer through the windows, no Claire in sight. Opening the door, my stomach drops upon settling my sights on the corner of her phone case peeking out from under my jacket she had been wearing. I reach forward and grip it in my hand. Everything is in its place—her ID, debit card, cash. If it's here, where is Claire?

Panic completely consumes me. The only way I could keep tabs on her was her phone's location service. Now, she could be anywhere. And that thought alone spikes a fear in me I've never known.

"Claire," her name is a whisper on my lips.

I punch in her passcode and dial the one person I'm praying she's with.

"What's up, bitch?" Rosie answers.

"Rose, is Claire with you?" I can barely hide the alarm in my voice.

Her tone immediately changes. "JJ? No, she's not here. Is everything okay?"

"Call me if you hear from her." I hang up the phone, not wanting to waste another second.

Claire isn't with her best friend. She's not with me. Where could she be?

If she didn't go to Rosie, she sure as shit didn't go to Pax's or

Holland's. And without her phone or any money, she couldn't have gotten too far.

The café, something inside me shouts.

She loves their coffee; maybe that's where she went to clear her thoughts before coming home.

I slam the door to the car shut and take off on foot. With all of the one-way streets and potholes, it'll be quicker if I make a beeline there, plus I can get a better look without being distracted by driving. I sprint straight there, taking the shortest route and peering down every single alley on the way. Each step closer, my soul pleads with the universe that she's okay. That she's sitting in the corner booth sipping a cup of cinnamon java, thinking of how mad she is at me. Because I'd have Claire pissed at me any day over the alternatives threatening to ruin me.

I can beg for her forgiveness, but I'll never forgive myself if something happens to her.

I grip the café's door and swing it open, rushing inside, frantically looking around, my eyes scanning every single patron.

The tired kid with the beanie stares at me. "Can I help you?"

"Claire, the girl I was in here with earlier." I rush over to him. "Have you seen her?"

He scratches his head, not seeming to understand the urgency of the situation.

His nonchalance annoys me to the point I grab the collar of his shirt and shake him. "Has she been in here tonight?"

"What the fuck, man?"

The door to the kitchen flaps open, and Luciano comes through. He seems less upset than he should that I'm assaulting his worker.

"What's the problem?" Luciano puts his hand on my shoulder.

I shrug it off. "Don't fucking touch me."

He puts his palms in the air. "I can't help you if you don't tell me what's wrong."

"Claire. Have you seen Claire?" I don't mind the eyes of the customers staring in disbelief at the sight of a psychotic man in their presence.

Luciano nods. "Yeah, she was in here. Got two coffees to go. Forgot her wallet. Said she had to get home. Sounded urgent."

I drop the kid's collar and pat the fabric down. "How long ago?"

If she was on her way home, I would have passed her on the way, right?

Luciano glances at his watch. "Maybe half an hour ago."

My shoulders slump. She definitely should have made it back by now. Is it possible she took another route? She's clueless with direction without her GPS.

Come on, Claire, where are you?

I leave the two of them and the rest of the café behind, popping out the front door and flipping my attention from left to right. I spot the sign for the university ahead. Maybe she went that way because it was familiar.

"Theo, wait," Luciano calls out.

I ignore him and take off in the direction I think she went. Scattered trash up ahead draws my attention. I run up to it, dropping to my knees when I realize what it is.

Two coffees. Just like Luciano had said.

I clutch my hand to my chest, afraid the world is going to fall out from under me.

"Over here." Luciano points to the street. "Tire tracks."

I drag my hands through my short hair. "It was Franklin, it had to have been Franklin," I mutter out loud, not caring if anyone else hears.

If Franklin has Claire, it might already be too late.

The memory of Griffin gripping Claire at the top of those stairs runs through my mind, the frightened look on her face as he pushed her closer to the edge. If I was only a minute longer, I would have lost Claire.

What if I've already waited too long?

I should have never let her walk away. I should have chased after her. Told her the truth right there. Made things right between us and never allowed her to wander off in the dark. Why did I think I should give her space, knowing damn well that Franklin was back in our lives?

"You're working with Franklin?" Luciano steps in front of me, demanding that I give him my attention.

I shake my head. "No. Well, not anymore." I pause. "Wait, you know Franklin?"

Luciano's fist tightens. "If Franklin took her, I know where she is. Come on."

And for some crazy fucking reason, I go with him, because right now, it's the only lead I have. It's foolish to trust this stranger, but he might be the only shot I have at getting to Claire before it's too late.

I trail him as he sprints back to the café and down the alley. An unnerving feeling trickles over me at the idea of going blindly into such a hauntingly familiar setting. I push it away, Claire being my sole focus. I will risk anything to get to her, to save her from whatever hell she's going through.

I should have told her about the note in our mailbox, about Josey showing up out of nowhere. Then she would have been on higher alert. Maybe she wouldn't have stormed off. She could have stayed with me, been mad at me at home, where she was safe.

I climb into the passenger seat of Luciano's black sedan. I ignore how nice it is, the deeply tinted windows and immaculate condition it's in. Café ownership isn't the most lucrative of professions. Maybe he's good at investing or into cryptocurrency. Whatever the hell that is.

He pushes a button to start the car, the engine roaring to life.

I hope this thing is as fast as it sounds and not a phony like those frat boy cars around town.

"How do you know Franklin?" I ask, despite being hesitant to know the answer.

Luciano peeks at me out of the corner of his eye. "He's blood."

I let my head fall back against the seat. Great. I just got into the car with my adversary's family. I should have just mailed myself to Franklin's doorstep with a glittery bow and saved Claire the misery of getting wrapped up in this nightmare.

"It's bad blood, though." Luciano grips the steering wheel with one hand and shifts aggressively with the other.

At least there's that. Perhaps we share a common enemy. Maybe this isn't my funeral after all. But what about Claire? What does Franklin have in store for her?

"He's forbidden from this territory. If he was in town, I'd know it." Luciano blazes through a red light, completely ignoring traffic laws. "Doesn't mean he didn't have someone do it for him, though."

If Franklin wanted to expose me, this is the perfect plan. Of course, because I'd do anything for her. But if there were no hints on how to find her, Franklin was probably more clueless than I thought. Which means that he's trying to get information out of Claire. And if I know her the way I think I do, there's no way in hell she'll give him any details on my whereabouts. As much as I would sacrifice for her, she'd do the same for me. Meaning if she doesn't spill soon, he'll end her life just for fun.

"How do you know Franklin?" Luciano repeats the same question I asked him.

I sigh, running my hand over my face. Where would I even begin? With Billy? No, that would show weakness, and without knowing a damn thing about Luciano, I don't want him to have any insight into what kind of person I am.

He skids the car sideways and onto a nearly hidden path, leading down rows of abandoned industrial buildings.

"It's a long story," I finally say.

"Keep an eye right, I'll look left." Luciano points to the access passages between the structures. He slams on the brakes and points ahead, where a lone van is parked in the distance.

Immediately, I hop out of the car and take off on foot.

Luciano catches up to me within a second, reaching behind him and pulling out a gun.

If he was going to kill me, he would have had the chance numerous times again. I allow the uncertainty of this man to be pushed aside as I run with all my might toward where my soul is screaming at me to go.

I only hope I'm not too late.

I hear her voice first, a soothing melody to my aching existence. But it's her words that breathe a new wave of fear in me.

"I'd rather die," she tells someone.

Followed by the uncanny sound of Franklin. "Very well. I'll find him with or without you."

I step into the open space, only a dozen feet away from my beloved. My heart seems to leap out of my chest at the sight of the weapon pointed in Claire's face.

I reach over, grabbing the gun from Luciano's hand, not a care in the world about what consequences could come from my actions. I point it at the man in front of Claire and just as he realizes there's a weapon aimed at him, I pull the trigger. The reverberation crashes through my wrist and up my arm, settling in my chest. My ears ring, the casing of the bullet rattles against the concrete floor. I shift my mark, pointing the end of my barrel at the other guy. I don't allow myself to think, I just do what I have to do, Claire's safety my only concern at the moment. I fire another shot, the loud noise secondary to everything else.

I glance at the screen in his grasp as it falls to the ground with the man's now lifeless body. Franklin's face pressed up close to get a better look, in total disbelief of what he's witnessing. I rush over, take one look at the still connected call and aim the gun one more time.

"You'll pay for this." I don't give Franklin time to react before I shoot the tablet and end any chance he has of saying a damn thing to me.

I turn around, dropping to my knees and grabbing Claire's face in my hands. Her eyes are pressed shut, her hair caked to her face with a mixture of blood and snot.

"Claire, I'm here." I hold my breath and frantically wait for some kind of response.

Did the man get off a shot before I could finish him? Or maybe his finger pulled the trigger in his final moments?

Slowly, she peeks through her lids at me. Her cheeks are swollen on both sides, a massive cut on her lip. If I hadn't already killed the two men who did this to her, I'd torture them until they begged me to end their lives. Now, it's Franklin who has to pay for what he's done to Claire.

"Johnny." Claire lifts her gaze to meet mine. A tear rolls down her cheek. "Are you really here?"

I quickly get to work untying the binds that hold her in place. "I'm here. I'm here. You're safe now. I'm here." I help her from the chair and bring her to my chest.

"Johnny? I thought your name was Theo?" Luciano whips his head toward me.

"I…" I really don't care what he thinks. The only thing on my mind is that Claire is safe. That I found her. That she's in my arms.

I hold her tightly against my chest, not wanting to ever let her go.

Claire grips me with an equal intensity. Her bloodied face pressed into me. "I'm sorry," she mumbles.

"Shh." I kiss the top of her head. "It's my fault. I'm sorry. I'm so sorry, Claire."

Rage, unlike anything I've ever known threatens to

completely unhinge me. Franklin will pay, if it's the last thing I do. It's one thing to fuck with me, but to hurt Claire? He has no idea the beast he's unleashed.

My gaze flits to the bodies lying on the floor, dead at my hand. Not a bit of remorse or regret. Just cold fury.

"Get out of here." Luciano takes the gun near my feet. "Use my car. I'll handle all of this." He pulls his phone out of his pocket and pushes a button. He presses it to his ear, "Five-oh-four. Mmhm. IDB." Luciano disconnects the call and hands me his keys. "Seriously, go."

And for the second time tonight, I put my faith in this complete stranger and hope like hell he doesn't prove me wrong in trusting him.

CLAIRE - 18

I thought I was going to die, and my last thoughts were of all that I would be leaving behind, most importantly, the man that holds my heart in the palm of his hand.

My face aches, and yet, all that's on my mind is the beautiful being in front of me.

Johnny dabs at my cheek with a towel, wincing like it hurts him more than it does me. I smile, knowing all too well exactly what he's going through. Every single time another mark was left on his body, a piece of me was lit on fire with a rage to inflict twice as much injury on the person who did it.

Sadness consumes Johnny's features as he delicately tries to clean me up.

I grip his hand, stopping his motion. "Johnny..." I force him to meet my gaze. I'm sure I look like shit, but I need him to understand. "None of this was your fault. I can *feel* it—you blaming yourself."

His jaw tightens, his demeanor still solid. "I shouldn't have let you go."

At this, my lips turn up. "You think you could have stopped me?"

Johnny tilts his head. "Claire, I'm serious. I...I should have told you."

Ah, the thing he's been hiding from me. His secret.

He runs his hand along his short hair—that old habit he still hasn't broken. If we ever make it out of this chaos, I hope for his sake that he can grow it out again.

"I need to tell you something, too." My voice cracks, but I can't keep this mountain of deceit between us any longer. "A few things, actually."

I've almost lost Johnny more times than I'd like to admit. If a war is on the horizon, I want to go into it on the same page, with everything out in the open. Even if he decides to hate me, I'll stand by him in this next chapter, fighting to free him from that sick monster once and for all.

But where do I start? With Luciano, or with Griffin? Both secrets are massive, and I'm not sure which one to lead with. The two of them could ruin us, but it could wreck us more if I continue to keep them from him.

"Whatever it is, Claire..." Johnny tucks my still gross hair behind my ear. "We'll get through it, okay? You can tell me anything."

My heart clenches.

He means well, but what if the truth is too tough to handle? What if it's more than he bargained for? What if he thinks *I'm* the villain in this story?

That's a reality I will have to face, because Johnny deserves better than this, better than the lying by omission. He's given me plenty of opportunities to choose my own destiny—to decide whether or not I wanted to stick around through all of the turmoil. I owe him that choice, too.

"The morning of my birthday..." Somehow, this moment is more terrifying than when I was staring down the barrel of that gun. Losing Johnny is a greater loss than dying. "I went to the hospital."

Johnny shows no reaction, just waits for me to continue.

"To see Griffin."

Finally, a bit of confusion as his brows bunch together.

"I...I couldn't go another day with him still out there. Alive." I let out a breath, the weight of what I'm about to say growing heavier and lighter all at once. "I poisoned him, Johnny. With a lethal dose of Tetrahydrozoline. That's why Griffin is dead—because I killed him."

Tears well in my eyes, but not because of what I did, because I don't know how Johnny will react.

"Claire." My name is a whisper on his lips. "Why?"

"I had to break free of him." I sniffle. "I couldn't allow him to continue to control me. To potentially wake up and hurt anyone else. To come between us. I couldn't stomach the idea of him walking free."

Johnny's emerald eyes flit back and forth between mine. "Claire." He cups my face between his hands with such a gentleness like I may break at his touch.

This is the moment I lose him. The one where he tells me I'm just as bad as Griffin, as Franklin. That he can't be with someone who could do something so very cruel. The last time I'll get to be this close to him, to feel his warm skin on mine.

Instead, his words surprise me.

"You are so brave."

My lips part, total disbelief washing over me. Brave? What I did was out of cowardice. *Fear.*

"Today, every day since I've known you, you continually surprise me with how fearless you are." Johnny pauses. "You're stronger than you think. Stronger than I give you credit for. Which is why I should have told you...I should have told you that on New Year's Eve, when I went out to check the mail, there was a note inside. From Franklin. I thought I could handle it on my own." He lowers his gaze for a second. "But I was wrong to keep that from you. I know that now. And I'm so sorry."

After what I just told him, *he's* the one apologizing?

"You were only doing what you thought was right." Because that's the same rationale I've told myself to excuse the withholding of information from each other.

"That's not all." Johnny lowers his hands to rest them on top of mine.

"Josey," I say with a sigh.

He blinks up at me. "How did you know?"

I clench my jaw, my memory flitting to earlier when I was kidnapped and tortured for information that I would rather die than give up. "Franklin."

"I'm going to make him pay for what he did to you."

I bring my fingers to his face, running them along his brow and across his cheek, feeling the raised skin where scars remain. "We. *We* are going to make him pay."

"Together," he sighs.

And although I've told him one truth, I have to admit the other before we can continue with our quest for vengeance. It was difficult to spit the first out, but it's nothing compared to the bomb I'm about to drop.

"There's something else." I go to bite at my lip, realizing all too late that it's busted.

"Oh, baby." Johnny snatches the towel and rests it at the bottom of my mouth.

"I understand if you hate me for what I'm about to tell you. I should have never gone behind your back."

Johnny stares into my eyes. "You're telling me now, and that's all that matters. I'm just as guilty, so how could I hate you? No more secrets, okay?"

I nod and swallow, forcing the words to come to me. "Remember when I told you about the food allergy thing?"

"Yeah?"

"Well, I lied. It was actually an ancestry test."

"Okay...?"

A knock rattles our front door, causing us both to flinch.

My heart nearly jumps out of my chest from the intrusion and the confession I was about to make.

Johnny sucks in a breath and presses his finger to his lips. "Shh." He tiptoes to the door and peers through the peephole. His shoulders relax slightly, and he glances back at me before opening it up.

"How did you get in here?" Johnny keeps his foot firmly pressed against the bottom of the door so it can't be opened any further.

"I own the building." The sound of Luciano's voice flutters over to me.

Of course he does. What isn't this man involved with?

"Can I come in?"

What weirdly convenient timing.

"Now?" Johnny tries to hide the annoyance in his voice, but he doesn't do a very good job.

"No, tomorrow." I can almost hear Luciano rolling his eyes from here. "Yes, now. Why else would I have asked?"

Johnny lets out an exaggerated breath and slides his shoe away, shutting the door to unlatch the security chain and opening it wide.

Luciano strolls in, shifting his gaze all around while making his way toward me. "I know a guy." He points at my face. "I can have someone look at that."

"I'm fine." Although, it really does feel like I got hit by a fucking truck. Can't say I've ever been punched in the face by a man or pistol-whipped before. I guess there's a first time for everything. And hopefully a last.

"What are you doing here, Luciano?" Johnny comes over and

stands in front of me, like he's protecting me from any potential threat.

Luciano sits down on the chair opposite of me, making himself right at home. "I need to know what I'm dealing with here. Clearly, you and Franklin have some kind of feud. I'm just trying to put all the pieces together. What's a guy like him have against someone like you?"

"The details aren't important." Johnny remains firm in place.

I raise my hand to rest it on his back. "Hey," I say calmly. "Sit." I manage to tug him down next to me.

Still, he pivots himself like a shield across me.

Luciano adjusts the cuffs of his black dress shirt. "I just disposed of two bodies for you. The least you could do is not act like I'm the dangerous person here."

I wrap my fingers around Johnny's, hoping it anchors him in this unsteady time.

"I worked for him, and then I didn't. He didn't exactly take my parting very well, tried to kill me." Johnny raises his shirt to show Luciano the scar on his torso. "I took the opportunity to fake my death, and here we are."

Luciano leans forward. "He put a hit out on you?"

"Why is that surprising to you? I thought you knew Franklin."

"Oh, I know him all right." Luciano shifts his gaze to me and then back to Johnny. "You two haven't *talked* yet, have you?"

I speak up. "We haven't exactly had the moment." I circle my finger around my face. "With this going on and all."

Johnny tenses beside me. It's one thing for me to have a secret, but to share one with this stranger, it's probably enough to unhinge him.

"What is it?" Johnny turns toward me.

"Well, um..." I point to Luciano. "He's part of your family tree."

There, I said it.

Johnny looks at Luciano. "What, like an uncle or something?"

Luciano runs his hand through his hair, the dark locks billowing in response.

"Actually." I brace for the bomb that I'm about to detonate. "He's your father."

Johnny rocks his head back and forth slowly. "No."

Luciano sits there, waiting for the shock to wear off. But something like this, on top of everything else that's happened, could take Johnny a while to process.

"Wait." Johnny scratches his temple. "If this is true." He stares at the man with a striking resemblance of him. "And you're my…dad." He emphasizes the last word like it might bite him. "What does that make me to Franklin?"

Now I'm the one thrown for a loop. What does Franklin have to do with any of this?

Luciano sighs. "His nephew."

I sit up straighter, trying to get around Johnny to get a better view of Luciano. "He's your brother?"

Luciano nods. "Unfortunately. Yes."

I am at a complete loss for words. Never in a million years did I imagine taking that small sample of Johnny's DNA would result in finding a birth father, let alone forever linking him to the man who tried to kill him. The sick fuck who almost ruined Johnny's life. Who was going to have a bullet blasted into my head a few hours ago because I wouldn't give him the information he wanted.

Nephew.

Wasn't that the same thing Franklin said about Josey? Which would either make Johnny and him brothers…or cousins. Either way, the plot thickens with them somehow being related, too.

JOHNNY - 19

"Honestly, Claire. I'm not mad."

She reaches out to stop me from pacing back and forth. "J. You've barely said a word since last night. Sure, you're here, you haven't left or kicked me out. But we have to talk, please. This silence is driving me insane."

I face her, seeing the hurt that runs much deeper than the damage Franklin's men caused. I've stayed with her every second since I found her in that abandoned building, afraid if I don't keep her within arm's reach, something terrible will happen.

Everything keeps falling apart, and the one thing I refuse to let go of is her.

"I'm not going to *kick you out*. This is *our* home. You." I press my finger to her chest. "And me."

A quiet resolve settles over her. Did she really think I'd bail on her? Yeah, I'm freaking out. About Franklin. Luciano. Literally, all the shit that's happening. But choosing to walk away from her because she was looking out for me? That would be foolish.

I absolutely wish she would have told me the truth, but I understand why she didn't.

Our bond may be deep, but our relationship is still fresh. We're figuring each other out. This is just part of the process. Good things don't come easy, and what Claire and I have, it's better than great.

What happened was not betrayal, and for that, I refuse to allow it to get between us.

If only I could figure out how to articulate all of this to her while managing the shit storm that keeps coming our way.

After Luciano left last night, I took Claire into our bathroom and finished tending her injuries as best as I could. I drew a warm bath and helped her undress and slink down into it. She had asked me to join her, and with my heart still aching from nearly losing her, I removed my clothes and slid in behind her. Her head had rested against my chest, and I fought to balance feeling so incredibly lucky for this beautiful angel in my presence and so fucking infuriated that I allowed her to get hurt.

I held her until it was time to get out and dry off, and even then, I made sure she was moisturized and that her hair was combed. I carefully slipped one of my T-shirts over her head and let her borrow a pair of my boxers because I thought it would be the most comfortable option. I tucked her into our bed and climbed in with her, desperate to show her how sorry I am.

I didn't sleep a wink, my mind wandering between rage and regret, fluttering every now and then to utter confusion.

I have a dad. Well, I knew I did, I just had no clue who he was, or that he was alive.

I thought it was just me, my mom's death leaving me on my own. I have my cousin, but that was it. He was never around. And from what I knew, his family was long gone, too. It wasn't really something we talked about, since we were too busy trying to figure out how to fend for ourselves. I had a strange childhood, one I wouldn't wish on anyone else—another reason why I was so adamant about Billy staying as far away from Franklin as possible. At least I managed to succeed at something.

Questions rattle my brain. Like the major one—why did Luciano fail to ever be a part of my life?

Plus, who the hell is he?

The dude is clearly loaded. He owns a café, which is more than likely a front for whatever criminal enterprise he's running. Diner owners don't have guys on call for body disposal.

He's related to Franklin. They're brothers.

Does that mean Luciano is the other side of the same coin?

And how does Josey know him?

Luciano mentioned them having bad blood—what does that mean?

"Johnny." Claire snaps her fingers in front of my face. "You zoned out again." She frowns, which comes out even sadder with the condition she's in. Swollen, puffy, redness turning into various shades of bruising, butterfly bandages holding together the cuts. "Did you sleep at all?"

It's difficult to even look at her. Not because I can't stomach stuff like that; I've definitely had my own fair share of bloody noses and busted lips—but the fact that it's Claire, my sweet girl. It makes me want to rush out of this apartment and rip apart every single person standing between me and Franklin and then slowly torture him, ensuring he feels every ounce of pain I can possibly inflict on him.

I was never a violent person. Not until I had something worth fighting for.

Now? There's no stopping what I would do to get even with him and anyone who ever dared lay a finger on her.

"Yeah, a little bit." We both know that's a lie.

I glance at my watch, the secondhand ticking by slowly while we wait for Luciano to show back up.

He had said he had some calls to make, some things to arrange, and that he'd be here at nine in the morning to regroup and figure out a plan of action.

I hate staying cooped up, but it makes the most sense at the moment. It's safer here, since Franklin clearly doesn't know where we are.

We can't risk exposing ourselves—not yet.

The only upper hand we have is that Franklin hasn't figured out my location. He made that clear when he tried to torture it out of Claire last night.

"Are you hungry?" Claire walks over to the kitchen and opens up the fridge. "I can make you breakfast."

It's then that I see her, truly see her. The kindness of her pouring out. The concern she has for me when she's been through hell herself. Not for a second has she shown weakness, despite terrible things happening to her. She almost died, and she's trying to make sure I eat.

What did I ever do to score such a beautiful soul?

"Come here." I hold out my arms and go over to her, pulling her in and nudging the refrigerator door shut with my hip. "I should be taking care of you. Not the other way around." I plant my lips on the top of her head, savoring her sweet scent.

She opens her mouth to respond but a knock thuds against the door.

I lower my hands to her shoulders and hold her at an arm's length, peering into her eyes. "It should be Luciano, but if it's not, you remember the plan?"

Claire swallows and nods, grabbing a butcher knife from the block and backing herself toward the window with our fire escape access.

It's something we practiced a few times at each of our new homes, just in case someone came for us. And now that the threat seems very real, so does the need to use our exit strategy.

I glide across the room, making sure not to make a sound on

my way to the front door. I hold my breath and peer through the peephole, relief washing over me when I see Luciano nonchalantly picking at the cuticle on his middle finger. I scan the hallway, my heart picking up its pace when I see Josey is leaning against the wall.

Luciano didn't mention Josey coming with him. And from what Claire mentioned, Franklin had him followed. Surely Luciano wouldn't be dumb enough to expose me like this, would he?

He might be my biological father, but he owes me no loyalty. He could easily throw me under the bus and go on with his life like nothing happened at all.

But I know Josey. I trust him. And he wouldn't do me like that…I don't think.

I crack open the door without sliding off the chain and keep my foot firmly in place. It's not much, but it would be enough to give Claire the chance to escape if they forced entry.

"Were you tailed?" I say through the small opening.

Luciano rolls his eyes. "You think this is my first rodeo?"

How am I supposed to know? I just met this dude.

I narrow my gaze, not appreciative of his condescending tone.

He sighs, and Josey pops around to step in front of him.

"That's what took us so long. Lucy picked me up, and we had to drive around like idiots making sure we were good. Took the service entrance, no cameras, no eyes. I wouldn't do you dirty, kid." Josey grabs a large duffel bag from the floor and slings it over his shoulder, then picks up a drink carrier with what I assume is Claire's kryptonite.

I sigh and shove the door shut to unlock it then swing it wide.

Luciano barrels in, acting like he owns the place. I guess in his case, he does.

"These apartments could definitely use some remodeling." He glances around.

"Let's worry about that another day." Josey hands me the drinks and a paper bag I didn't realize he was holding then walks over to the couch, dropping the massive duffel with a clunk.

Claire comes around to my side, still clutching the butcher knife in her hand. She puts her arm around me but stays firm in place, a reminder of how strong she is in the face of evil.

"Damn, girl, you've seen better days." Josey scrunches up his face at Claire. "You okay?"

She nods stiffly. "You should see the other guy."

A bit of dark humor, I like it.

"I did, actually." Josey reaches forward and slides a cup from the holder, popping the top and taking a sip. He winces. "Shit, I must have got one of yours." He pushes the thing toward me and takes another, making sure to check the lids this time. He settles into a free spot and throws his arm around the back.

Luciano clears his throat. "Coffee." He gives one to Claire and takes one for himself. He points to the paper bag. "Donuts."

Claire slides away from me and returns with a stack of napkins.

Josey is the first to grab one, clearly being the ice breaker of our awkward group.

It's been less than twenty-four hours and I have no idea how to act around this man who happens to be my father. Who is also some kind of criminal and happens to be related to the man who would stop at nothing to end my life.

Luciano starts. "I have eyes all over the city. Franklin won't get in without me knowing. For now, we're in the clear, but that doesn't mean his mercenaries aren't already in place. We have to be vigilant." He turns to Claire. "After what happened to you, it's best to stay put for now. This is war, and we can't afford to make any mistakes."

Josey wipes his face and leans forward. "Listen, this is great, and I'm totally on board with whatever is about to happen, but will someone clue me in on what the fuck this is?" He points between me and Luciano. "When did you two become best buds?"

I raise my hand to my hair, that stupid habit of mine. I catch Luciano doing the same damn thing out of the corner of my eye.

"Theo—excuse me—*Johnny*, is my son," Luciano says matter-of-factly.

Josey's brown eyes go wide, and he nearly spits out his coffee. "What?"

"It's true," Claire assures him.

"Wait?" Confusion settles over Josey. "Does that mean…?"

Luciano lets out an exasperated breath. "You're cousins, yes. Now, can we get back to business?"

"Holy shit, man." Josey hops up from his seat and grabs my arm, pulling me into a breath-squeezing hug. "I knew I liked you for a reason."

"The feeling is mutual." I slap his back, the same thought running through my head. I've always had this weird trust in Josey, despite not really knowing why. He's always been nice to me, and we've had this sort of unspoken comradery.

My phone buzzes in my pocket, which is cause for alarm considering the only person who talks to me on a daily basis is in this very room.

I pull it out, the text from my contact back home sending my heart rate a bit higher.

"He's on his way," I say to anyone who might be listening.

"How do you know?" Luciano stares up at me.

"I have a reliable source." I pause and add, "He left an hour ago."

Luciano's gaze seems to dart away, like he's lost in thought. "He's on a private jet. Estimated four hours travel time, giving us three until he arrives. If I'm right, he's flying into a small airport right outside my jurisdiction. I'll make a few calls to see if I can get exact details on tracking. If we're going to do this, we'll have to attack the second he lands."

"Isn't that against your agreement?" Josey breaks through Luciano's planning.

"He already broke it when he tried to kill my son."

A chill goes up my back. I don't know if it's the usage of the word, or the sheer determination on Luciano's face to end Franklin. He might be doing this for his own reasons, but the fact that he wants him dead almost as much as I do forms a strange bond between us.

It may be temporary, but it's there, nonetheless.

"What do we do?" Claire readies herself next to me. Her face is swollen and bruised, and I'm sure causing her a great deal of pain. Still, she puts that all aside to prepare herself for battle against the man who keeps trying to ruin us.

Luciano nods at Josey, signaling him to open up the bulky black bag.

With a hint of excitement about him, Josey complies, unzipping it and pulling out a shotgun onto our living room table and reaches in for another. A pistol this time, with a tactical-looking scope secured to the top. Then, two smaller revolvers. He places them all gently side by side and keeps going back for more.

"Dibs on this one," he says as he lugs out an AR-15.

Luciano rolls his eyes. "You're a child."

Josey continues to pull weapons out of the bag. Knives, more handguns, even a few smoke bombs.

"There's plenty more where that came from," Luciano tells us. "I'm assembling a team to back us, and I'm sure Franklin has already done the same. He's ruthless, but he's predictable. That will work to our advantage."

Claire reaches forward, hovering over the smaller guns and picking one up.

The rest of us stay quiet as she examines it.

She confidently thumbs a button near the trigger, dropping the magazine into her other palm. She grips the slide and pulls it back, eyeing the barrel and then releasing it. Claire shoves the magazine back into the gun and sizes up the weight of it in her hand. She narrows her gaze along the rear sight and then lowers it, finally looking at the rest of us. "I'll take this one...if that's okay?"

Luciano chuckles and splays out his hands. "By all means." He latches onto a smaller, more compact one and extends it to her. "This one will conceal nicely, too."

Claire takes it from him, repeating the same motions she had done on the other one. "Thanks."

"You didn't tell me you were dating a badass." Josey brings his coffee to his lips, reminding me that I have one of those, too. "Although, I should have known when she slapped the shit out of me."

I catch Luciano raising an eyebrow out of the corner of my eye.

"Is that so?" Luciano seems intrigued.

Claire shrugs, blowing it off like no big deal. She tucks the bigger of the guns into the back of her waistband. "Don't expect an apology out of me. You had it coming."

I can't help but be proud as hell. Claire is a remarkable individual, continually surprising me with her resiliency and loyalty.

A grin spreads across Josey's cheeks. "I did, didn't I?"

"If you need to make any further preparations, now is your time to do so. I'll be back for you at the top of the hour." Luciano checks his expensive-looking watch. "You have roughly twenty-two minutes." He stands and focuses on Josey. "Come on, you buffoon."

Josey slaps Luciano's shoulder. "Lucy, you know I'm your favorite nephew."

Luciano straightens out his shirt. "You're my *only* nephew, Joseph."

The banter between them is a welcomed distraction from the clock ticking down, a steady reminder that the end is coming. My only hope is that we're the ones who get to call the shots.

The two of them exit through the front door, leaving me and Claire alone.

"Are you ready for this?" I ask her.

A wildness flickers in her eyes, telling me all I need to know without saying a word.

CLAIRE - 20

Is it bad that I'm not nervous?

I'm not scared. There is no fear coursing through me.

Only rage. Anger. The thirst for sweet revenge.

I used to be afraid of the world. I allowed people to walk all over me, control me, take me for granted. But now? Now I've shed that unwanted skin, and transformed into a person who looks scary situations in the face without a bit of hesitation.

There's a sort of calmness about giving in and overcoming the things holding you back.

It's probably reckless, completely foolish of me. But I do so without reservations, because the only way we're going to take Franklin down is if we refuse to cower to his intimidation tactics.

I've had enough of him calling the shots.

Luciano, in the passenger seat of this blacked-out SUV, reaches behind him and pulls out a handgun. He turns and holds it out to Johnny. "Here."

Johnny wavers. "I already have one."

"I insist." Luciano nudges it forward.

The shots being fired last night replay in my memory. I had clenched my eyes shut, thinking I was going to die, only to open them to see my beautiful man kneeling before me, both men who kidnapped me lying on the floor of that building, dead. A gun next to Johnny's foot. The one he must have used to kill the two people who took me. The one Luciano must be trying to give him now.

"I'll take it if you don't want it," Josey chimes in.

Luciano fires him a death glare.

Josey raises his large arms. "Just saying."

Johnny decides to grab the gun, probably to settle the tension of the offering. "Thanks."

Luciano nods and turns back to the road.

Another SUV like ours is in front of us, and another follows behind. Both of them are full of armed men that Luciano was able to scrounge up on short notice, only confirming my suspicions that he's in the same line of business as Franklin. I just hope like hell he's a better man, at least for Johnny's sake.

I'm sure learning he had a father was difficult enough to handle, but if Luciano turns out to be the same as Franklin, I'm afraid of how Johnny will react. He's already been through so much. He deserves to have some kind of silver lining in his life. It can't all be one bad thing after another. Johnny has sacrificed everything to do the right thing; it's time for the right thing to finally happen to him.

We pull onto a gravel road, following the lead of the first vehicle in our entourage.

Johnny's hand grips mine tightly.

I take my free hand and double-check that my weapons are in place. It's not like they could get up and walk away, but in this kind of situation, it's better safe than sorry. I accidentally elbow Josey and mumble, "Sorry."

"You nervous?" Josey turns his attention from out the window to me.

"Not at all."

"Good." He winks at me. "You got any older, crazy friends like you running around out there?"

Johnny tilts his head toward Josey. "Seriously? Right now?"

Josey shrugs. "What better time?"

Our driver, a middle-aged guy who hasn't said a word this whole trip, presses on the brakes, slowing us down and pulling in next to the other SUV. A large building, I'm assuming a hanger for an airplane, blocks our view of the runway.

Luciano points ahead. "They'll taxi over there." He moves his hand. "We'll be waiting over there." He glances into the back at us. "Any questions?"

I look to Johnny and then at Josey, neither one of them saying a word.

"Very well." Luciano hops out, which triggers everyone from the other two vehicles to disperse, too.

Johnny climbs out of his side, holding his hand to help me onto the ground. He'd rather me not be here, that much is clear, but he knows damn well I'm going to see this thing through with him. We may not have started this journey together, but we're sure as shit going to finish it side by side.

I catch sight of a familiar face—that kid from the diner, the one with the beanie, who seems entirely too young to be here. We make eye contact, but he carries on without any sign of wavering. He doesn't seem bothered by the condition of my face, unlike the others, who flinch a little when their gaze lands on me. It makes me wonder what kind of things this kid has seen to make him so blasé.

It's not that I want his pity—hell, I appreciate the fact that he carried on with no concern. It's just that I hope he doesn't lose himself to this kind of life. The darkness that will take over and consume him with no disregard for his humanity. I don't wish that kind of thing on anyone.

One by one, we make our way over to where Luciano had

told us to wait. He does some elaborate hand signals and directs a few of the armed men here and there.

It suddenly dawns on me that I'm the only female here. Not that that's a bad thing. It just goes to show what kind of world I've found myself in.

Luciano takes point at one corner of a building, and Josey makes his way to the other.

"Stay behind me," Luciano tells me and Johnny.

A silent fury bubbles up within me at the command.

Johnny tenses like he feels the same exact way.

After everything that Franklin has put Johnny through, it's no wonder we both want to shove everyone aside and handle this situation on our own.

The one thing stopping us is wanting to actually make it out alive.

We've had too many close calls, and ending Franklin will be for nothing if we don't make it through to the other side still breathing.

I hold a pistol firmly in my grasp, careful to maintain trigger control. I say a mental *thank you* to my father for those random shooting range sessions we had taken when I was a child. Who would have known that they would come in handy so much in my adult life?

Luciano glances at his watch. "Any minute now," he whispers back at us.

Like clockwork, we hear the sound of whirring somewhere above us in the sky.

My heart picks up its pace, ready for this to finally be over. In a perfect world, I'd tie Franklin to a chair and torture him until he begged for reprieve, but an ambush and a bullet to the head will do, too.

Just as long as he's the one who dies when this is all said and done.

A screech comes from the runway as the plane touches

down, the brakes locking up to slow its speed.

Luciano holds his hand up, all of us staying in place, waiting for his sign to move.

It's strange to think that a few days ago, we barely knew this man, and now he's leading the attack against Franklin, his own brother.

The plane continues to taxi, moving to the exact location Luciano said.

Finally, it stops completely.

I can barely make it out from my spot tucked behind him and Johnny. I strain to peer around them, but Johnny is like a shadow in front of me, moving when I do to block me from harm's way. I'm not even sure if he realizes he's doing it, or if it's just a reflex reaction.

After a minute, the door to the aircraft finally opens with a whooshing sound.

A single man steps outside of the plane, walking down the small set of stairs without a care in the world. Perhaps he's the pilot? It's difficult to tell from my vantage point.

Luciano drops his arm, a slew of men running around us with their guns drawn.

The guy immediately throws his hands up in the air and stops in his tracks. "Don't shoot."

Johnny and I take off behind the crowd, rushing to catch up with Luciano and Josey.

A few of our guys rush into the belly of the plane and come back out.

"Clear," one of them says.

Luciano curses under his breath. He points his gun at the man's head. "Where is he?"

The pilot shakes his head. "I don't know. It's just me."

"Why are you here?" Luciano stares at the man such intensity, proving just how very similar he is to Franklin.

"I—" the guy struggles to speak under the pressure of the

many weapons trained in his direction. "I got paid, twenty large. To fly here. I didn't ask questions. I need the money. My kid has this medical—"

Luciano cuts him off. "That's enough." He looks to one of his men, "Get his phone."

The pilot's eyes glisten, "Please, I have…"

Luciano interrupts him again, and just when I think he's about to shoot this guy because he can, he motions at him. "Get out of here."

Making damn clear that he may be in the same line of business as Franklin, and they may share blood, but they are not cut from the same cloth.

And that alone gives me hope that Johnny may be able to have a relationship with this man after all.

Luciano turns toward the gathering group of men. "Tear that plane apart. I need any clue you can find." He flits his attention toward me and Johnny. "He knew you had a spy on him. And he played it right into his hand. We've been busy orchestrating this, distracted." He hesitates before finishing, "I wouldn't be surprised if he's already here."

If he snuck in without Luciano finding out, that could mean that he's anywhere.

No place is safe. No one is safe. It's only a matter of time until he comes for us.

Until he comes for Johnny.

"Hey…" I sit on the edge of this unfamiliar bed, watching Johnny pace across the room Luciano gave us to hide out in. "Come here." I pat the lavish comforter next to me.

Johnny pauses, his gaze meeting mine. His eyes are full of

immense worry that will only be erased when this is all said and done.

I can't rid him of that apprehension, but maybe I can take his mind off of them for a little while.

Johnny lowers his butt onto the mattress, his shoulders slump despite the tension flowing through him. "I have a bad feeling."

I place my hand on his arm. "We're going to get through this."

I hate how difficult it is to hide my own uncertainty.

He turns toward me, doing his best not to flinch at the sight of my face. "I can't believe I let that happen to you."

"Johnny, stop. Stop beating yourself up about something you ultimately had no control over." I inch closer to him. "Let's focus on the here, the now."

Johnny tilts his head. "Claire..."

I press my finger to his lips to quiet him. "No. I don't want to hear anything else. All I want to do is get lost in the only thing that truly matters to me in this world. *You.* There's no point in focusing on anything else when there's nothing we can do right now."

He sighs, his gaze carefully fluttering over me.

"Give me that, at least for one last night."

Johnny rocks his head back and forth. "See, that's the thing, I can't stomach the thought of this being the end."

"Then don't." I graze my fingers along his cheek. "We're going to win this, no matter what it takes."

And maybe it's a stupid thing to say, but I refuse to give Franklin any more than he's already stolen from us.

"I love you." Johnny closes his eyes and leans into my touch. When he opens them, it's as though there's a fire behind them, sparking him to life.

I run my thumb across his bottom lip and bring my face

forward, pressing my mouth against his. If I'm careful, I can do so without bumping into my cut.

Johnny kisses me softly, paying special attention to my wound, but somehow intensifying the moment between us. He tilts his body, mine shifting back in response, giving him more space to climb on top of me. "Are you sure?" He breaks away and stares at me seriously.

I nod with absolute certainty. "Yes." I grip the hem of his shirt and pull it over his head, tossing it aside, running my fingers up his chest and then down to unbutton his jeans.

He hops off the bed and tugs them down, never once breaking eye contact with me as I slide out of my own bottoms, leaving me completely naked aside from my loose top.

Johnny grips my thighs and comes forward, his mouth hovering its way further and further up until he swirls his tongue over where my panty line would be. He inches closer, the build-up driving me wild.

I reach to grab onto his hair, annoyed with the shortness of it and the difficulty it poses on being able to navigate him where I want him more easily.

Anticipating my desire, he licks deeper, starting at my clit and gliding down, down, down. He brings his fingers closer, teasing my entry until I'm angling myself toward him greedily.

How is it possible that we've barely just started and I'm already dying for a release?

Johnny presses his index finger against my hole, and I rock my body onto it.

A moan escapes my lips, my head tilting back at the pleasure of the slightest penetration.

He obliges me by giving me another digit, curving them upward and putting gentle pressure on my g-spot.

I clench around him and he slows his movement, pulling them both out and dipping them into his mouth. I let out a frustrated sigh at having been so close, but I'm well aware Johnny knows exactly what he's doing.

This time, he fills me with three, a new wave of pleasure rippling through me at the resulting stretch and fullness. He continues to lick and suck my clit, dragging it carefully between his teeth and intensifying the feeling.

I grip the sheets and clench my jaw.

He slides his other hand up my thigh, positioning it right under my ass, his thumb caressing me in ways that only heighten my enjoyment.

When I initiated this sexcapade, my intention was to get his mind off things, but damn if he isn't completely consuming my every thought.

Johnny keeps this up for a few more minutes, bringing me closer to the edge and then pulling me back, with full and utter control over my climax. I no longer fight it; I embrace that I will come when he wants me to, despite the frustration it may cause.

Finally, he stops, breaking away completely and stroking himself with his soaked hand. He climbs his way up, shoving my shirt aside to take each of my nipples into his mouth and giving them some desired attention. I nearly come undone both times, and he's fully aware of it.

His mouth meets mine, and the taste of myself on his lips.

I kiss him deeply, reveling in the sting of my split lip. I spit onto my palm and reach down, gripping his hard cock, desperate to bring him pleasure, too.

I drag him to me, massaging and bringing him to my eager entrance.

"Claire, we don't have a..." He breathes against me.

And maybe because this might actually be the last time, or because I cannot possibly spend another second without feeling him inside me, I tell him, "I don't care."

I'm on birth control, and we don't have any other active

partners. There's no reason we can't live life on the edge in this moment of intimacy, when we are everywhere else.

Johnny must be on the same page as me, given the fact that he doesn't question any further. Instead, he positions himself in place and as slowly as humanly possible, inches himself into me.

I dig my nails into his back and spread my legs wider to give him more access. I savor this new sensation, wishing there was some way to freeze this moment in time, the one with our bodies intertwined, his gaze focused on me, nothing in the world except me and him.

He picks up his pace, cruising from a slow thrust to a deeper, steadier rhythm. "Is that okay?"

I huff a snort of disbelief and his eyes flutter shut at the resulting squeeze on him. "Yeah."

He grows inside of me, throbbing and filling me full of him.

I tighten around him, but I don't dare come, not yet, not until he wants me to. I ride that edge and fight the desire to throw myself over without him.

Johnny weaves his fingers through mine, dragging them over my head and holding onto them with one of his hands. He holds himself up with the other, but drops his face to my neck, kissing and swirling his tongue along my collarbone and up to my ear. He tugs on the lobe, breathing against the sensitive skin. Johnny slows down, lengthening his stride and tilting himself just right to hit my clit in the process.

I moan again, nearly losing this battle with myself.

"Let go," he whispers, thrusting into me again, with just the right amount of pressure to send me spiraling.

Johnny exhales and continues to plunge in and out, fierce in a way I've never experienced before.

My body ripples with an intense gratification, consuming me from head to toe as our orgasms go off in tandem, one being propelled higher by the other, forming a peak of beautiful rapture.

It lasts longer than I could have imagined, and honestly, even when he stops moving, I convulse with the aftershock of the high.

Johnny stays inside me while bringing his face over to mine, resting his lips against my mouth. "I love you."

I smile and sigh, never feeling anything more powerful than what I do for him. "I love you."

I don't know what this war will bring, but one thing is for damn sure, I would do anything for my man and will stop at nothing to bring him the victory and subsequent peace he so deserves.

JOHNNY – 21

I feel like everything is spiraling out of control. For the smallest moment, I thought I had a hold on the situation, but now it's like I'm walking through a constant minefield, wondering which step is going to cause a massive explosion.

Things were sketchy enough when Franklin was two thousand miles away, still unsure of whether or not I was alive. But with the momentary video chat where I killed two of his men, confirming his suspicions, he could be anywhere. Around any corner. Lurking in any shadow. Waiting, preparing, planning the perfect opportunity to strike.

I have no idea how to keep Claire safe when things are so fucking uncertain.

On the West Coast, I knew his hangouts, the places he frequented. I had a solid grasp of who was part of his organization. Out here? I'm totally blind to which moves he'll take, to the people he has on his payroll.

Luckily, my sperm donor is just as powerful as Franklin is, if not more.

For the last twenty-four hours, we've been tucked into one

of his safe houses. The only way in or out is with a retinal scan and a code that very few know. Luciano added us to the list and gave us access to our own side of the massive loft. He assured us that the windows were bulletproof, even if someone was able to get a shot off at this height, and that the place was pretty much impenetrable.

That's all fine for now, but eventually, we will have to leave.

Luciano scratches his beard and leans up against the doorframe. "I still haven't located Franklin." His green gaze meets mine and then shifts to the floor. "This is very unlike him. He is usually much more predictable."

I guess Luciano doesn't know Franklin the way that I do. Sure, most of his moves can be anticipated, but he's also completely irrational and impulsive. There is no rhyme or reason to some of the things he goes through with, other than to feed his twisted desires.

Claire's phone dings, and all three of us turn our attention toward the device.

She picks it up, her shoulders relaxing once her eyes settle on the screen. "It was just an email. From one of my professors."

I've forced Claire into a life where she has to lie to her teachers to excuse her absence. I hate myself for everything I've put her through, and if I don't figure out how to end this for good, all of this will have been for nothing. She deserves better than what I've given her, and I won't stop until I make sure that happens.

"I still don't understand why he's so hell-bent on killing you." Luciano crosses his arms. "I mean, to risk coming here, on my turf, to settle a petty dispute? We have people quit all the time. You don't see me chasing them down."

"It was never about Johnny quitting," Claire speaks up for me. "J was actually still technically working for him when he gunned him down."

"Then what was it?"

Claire meets my gaze and then looks to Luciano. "Johnny outsmarted him. He saw an opportunity to help someone, and he did. He basically sacrificed a year of his life to free this innocent person for no reason other than to do the right thing." Claire takes a breath, shaking her head. "J convinced everyone that he was this bad guy, and don't get me wrong, he did some bad shit, but it was the most selfless thing I've ever seen anyone do. And once Franklin realized Johnny had the upper hand, he did the only thing he could. He had him shot."

Luciano cuts in at this point. "Then you outsmarted him again when you faked your death. Making him look like a complete idiot."

I shrug. "In a nutshell."

Claire continues, "If we're being honest here, I think Franklin is weirdly intimidated by Johnny's altruism. Threatened even. Like this one person could potentially ruin whatever he has going. I don't think anyone has ever done what Johnny did and got away with it. So he's making a point to follow through with his threats, to keep his reputation intact."

"I could see that," Luciano adds.

"But what about you?" I ask the man offering us a safe haven. "You said there was bad blood?"

Luciano twists his foot into the floor and glances over his shoulder briefly. "This line of business definitely isn't for the faint of heart. But, to go about it the way Frankie does…it's wrong. I'm not saying I'm a better man than him, we just don't see eye to eye on the way we handle things. We never have. He was always competitive and so damn spiteful. Honest mistakes would turn into these huge pissing matches. It was childish, and absolutely reckless. Petty stuff, like I couldn't even show interest in a girl around him because he would stake this weird-ass claim.

"I tried and tried to keep the peace, but it got to the point where it was impossible. Nothing I could do was right. He got fucking mad over everything." He lets out a long breath. "I—uh, I had gained the east coast sector, and after that, there was no coming back. It didn't matter that we were blood, that we were brothers. There was no reasoning with him. One day, things escalated too far. People got hurt. Good people. I couldn't allow him to stay here and continue to fuck everything up. He went west, somehow weaseled his way into the position he's in now, and we've basically been rivals ever since."

I've been in denial about Luciano's *professional* life since the moment I caught wind of it being similar to Franklin's. He's my father. And to think that he could be this cruel person like Franklin—it turned my stomach. I couldn't fathom that I had been brought into this world by that kind of person. Not when everything I've done has been for the good of others.

But hearing the way Luciano talks about Franklin, about how he disagreed with his ways, to the point that he essentially disowned him, it gives me hope that perhaps I was wrong about the kind of man I worried Luciano was.

Sure, he's a criminal—but he is nothing like Franklin, and for that alone, I am grateful. Maybe there is a future for us after all.

Claire breaks the silence, keeping her sights trained on Luciano. "Sounds like Franklin saw a little bit of you in Johnny."

Is it possible we're more alike than I thought? There are definitely some striking physical similarities, but what if Franklin noticed it, too? I could have reminded him too much of his brother. The man he would never be. I threatened him because I showed him the error of his ways. That I was good, and he was evil.

And that in the end, I think deep down he knew I would win, just like Luciano had.

I'd like to think that I would have walked away from Franklin, gotten out from under his thumb, and gone my separate way. But in hindsight, I'm not sure if I could have allowed such a sick fuck to go free. It's possible that Franklin knew I'd come for him before I even did.

Claire's phone buzzes again, this time longer instead of the single vibration earlier.

She holds it out for me to see the screen. "It's Rosie. She's FaceTiming me."

"She's probably checking in to see how you are."

"Do I answer it?" Claire glances at me and then Luciano, then back to me.

"I don't see the harm in it," I tell her.

Claire slides her finger across to accept the call. She holds it out in front of her and allows it to connect. Within a split second, her expression shifts from a smile to something of utter terror.

"Claire," Rosie wails.

I rush over to Claire, taking her phone from her to get a better look at what could be causing her such alarm.

A spit-soaked rag dangles just below Rosie's mouth. Her blonde hair is matted to her mascara-stained cheeks. She's secured to a chair, her arms and legs in place the same way Claire's were last night.

Never in a million years did I think Franklin would go after Rosie, but I guess no one is safe when it comes to him. He went after who was important to me—Claire. And when I got Claire safely away from him, he did the same to her.

The screen pivots, a person coming into view.

The man behind this all.

Luciano rushes over but I hold out my hand to him.

He furrows his brows but complies with a subtle nod.

Franklin may hate us both, but I don't think he knows we're working together. And if we can maintain the slightest advantage against him, I'll graciously take it.

"Mr. Jones, what a pleasure." Franklin slides a butcher knife off a metal tray, twirling it gently in his hand. "So glad to see you alive and well." He exhales. "We haven't had a chance to catch up." Franklin stares into the camera. "How's the weather?"

I clench my jaw. "Let her go, Franklin." My gaze flicks to the doorway, where Josey has now taken up residency.

Franklin completely ignores my demand. "Yeah, it rained a bit back home on and off. Beats this cold, though."

"Tell me what you want." Although I know exactly what he's going to say.

Despite already having my attention, he lifts the blade toward Rosie, running the tip of it down the side of her temple. "Sure would be a shame to mark up another pretty lady's face."

My blood boils at the implication behind his words. He already did the unthinkable to the woman I love, there's no telling how far he'd take it with Rosie. She's just another disposable pawn in his gruesome game, and I'm not entirely positive she'll make it out of this alive.

I thought I had already put Claire through enough, but having her witness the brutal murder of her best friend? That would be a line crossed we could never come back from.

Franklin pulls the blade away and faces the camera again. "How about an even trade? You for her. Easy enough. Then we can chat in person."

"When and where?"

Claire tenses beside me, but I refuse to look her way. I can't allow my concentration to waver while the call is still connected.

"Good answer." Franklin grins a toothless grin. "You can bring Claire. I'd hate for Rosie here to have to walk home in the dark. I'll text you the details. And Johnny..." He waits until he has my full attention to continue. "You two come alone, or you don't come at all. If you bring anyone else, I'll carve this girl up like a pumpkin on Halloween."

And with that final threat, the call is disconnected.

"He's going to kill her." The words we are all thinking leave Claire's mouth first.

"I'm not going to let that happen." It's true, he really does want me, and I have a feeling this is one of those situations he's giving me that I can actually succeed at. Even if the prize at the end is my death.

Claire's best friend will not die because of me.

"You can't go." Claire tugs on my arm in an attempt to pull my attention to her.

Defeat crashes over me. I've always found a way to slip out of Franklin's grasp just in the nick of time. There has always been some kind of escape route in place. But now, I can think of none. I'll be walking right into his palm, with no means of a way out. For once, he finally outsmarted me and put me in a complete checkmate.

All that's left is finding the courage to say goodbye.

Slowly, I tilt my head toward her. My heart aching at the pain I've put her through since the moment I stepped into her life. I bumped into her that fateful night, knocking her down, and all I've done since is continue to ruin everything. I was a coward for not having the strength to stay away from her then. I was selfish and idiotic for thinking I could ever be the type of man that Claire deserves. We may have formed something beautiful and rare together, but at what cost?

I cannot allow my angel to fall.

"Don't look at me like that." Claire's bottom lip quivers.

"Like what?"

"Like you're about to say goodbye."

Luciano finally steps forward, metaphorically and literally putting his foot down. "No one, and I repeat *no one*, is saying goodbye."

"Yeah, what he said." Josey comes into the room, his muscles nearly bulging out of his T-shirt.

"There's no way around it," I tell them. "I've run countless scenarios through my head. The only way I can save Rosie is to give him what he wants. And once I'm there, there's no turning back. He won't let me escape for a second time."

"You stopped me from coming into view for a reason." Luciano stares at me intensely. "He doesn't know we're working together. He'd never see it coming."

"How does that help me, though? He said for us to come alone. I wouldn't put it past him to follow through with his threat if we do a damn thing to make him suspicious. I won't let Rosie get hurt."

"Wait, who's Rosie?" Josey rubs his chin.

Claire's phone goes off in my hand, the details Franklin promised beaming across the screen.

The wheels in Luciano's brain seem to start turning as a plan formulates in his head. "I have an idea."

CLAIRE – 22

If Rosie dies, I'm going to lose my mind. If it's Johnny instead, I'll still lose my mind. I should have known that I'd be putting her in danger by running back to my old life. I was foolish to think we'd actually get away. I underestimated just how far Franklin would take things to get his way.

Now, it feels like all hope is lost, and that there's no chance at saving any of us.

If we can get Rosie to safety, I'll stay by Johnny's side and go headfirst into whatever fate has in store for us. I refuse to walk away from him, no matter how difficult things become.

He is my person, the only reason I'm still here today.

It was never about owing him anything; it was that we solidified ourselves as one. We share our challenges, our successes, any hurdle or obstacle, and we rise to the top together.

Keeping secrets was stupid. We thought we were doing the right thing for each other, when in reality, the best thing we could have done was be honest. We're a team, and we've already overcome mountains. What's another impossible feat?

Johnny grips my hand firmly as we march down the dark street. He glances over at me, his eyes silently pleading with me to turn around, to go back. But he knows better. He wouldn't walk away, and neither will I.

The cold metal of the guns presses up against my bare skin under my shirt. Each step we take, we get closer to the possibility of death.

"This isn't right," Johnny says under his breath.

"I know."

He pauses under a dim section of the sidewalk. "What if it doesn't work?" His green gaze traces over me, sending those all too familiar butterflies dancing around my belly.

Even in the darkest of times, my love for him flourishes.

I graze his cheek with my hand and savor every detail of him that I can make out in the darkness of night. I run my thumb along his bottom lip, every single kiss replaying in my memory. "At least we'll have tried." And it might be an influx of desperation, but I tell him, "We're going to make it through this."

Because I can't accept the alternative. I refuse to think Johnny sacrificed everything for nothing. That we were placed in each other's lives only temporarily. There's more to our story than what we've already been through. There has to be a light at the end of this darkness.

If not for me, for him.

"I want to believe that." Johnny carefully raises his hand to my cheek, hesitating along the skin. "I'm sorry, Claire, for everything. For this..." He hovers over the wounds on my face, still aching from the beating from Franklin's goons. "For not being able to stay away from you when I knew I should have."

"Hey, you don't get to carry that burden. I regret nothing. Okay?" I stare into those beautiful emerald eyes. "I'd do it all over again if it meant being with you."

Maybe I'm foolish, but the time I've shared with Johnny has been the best moments of my life. And I truly think that in order to appreciate the good, you have to endure the bad. Our highs were higher because our lows were so damn low.

I stand on my tiptoes, sliding my arms around Johnny's neck and pulling him down into me. I don't care that he's afraid to kiss me with my injuries, I press my lips to his anyway.

I can be beaten, but I will not be broken. If I'm going to die tonight, I'm going to cherish these final moments with my man. Almost dying after fighting with him was awful. I'm going to make sure he knows how much I love him.

Johnny is gentle, extra careful not to apply too much pressure. His touch is soft and delicate, just like he has been our entire relationship. Never once did he show an ounce of aggression or control over me. It's not that he isn't capable of it; he just reserves it for anyone who threatens someone he cares about. He is fierce, and strong, but he is kind and thoughtful.

Johnny is a man that I am grateful for having known. To have shared my life with, even if for such a short period.

He gave me the strength to step into the woman I am today.

"I love you, Claire Cooper," he whispers against my mouth.

"I love you, Johnny Jones."

Johnny rests his forehead against mine. "Together?"

It's as though he finally realizes the magnitude of my love for him—the lengths I would go to have him with me.

I smile through the pain, both physical and internal. "You're stuck with me, remember?"

Johnny lets out a breath, breaking away and studying me intently. "Yeah." He rocks his head back and forth gently, a sort of disbelief in his expression.

I weave my hand around his, uniting us again. We are stronger together, and I want to make damn sure that Franklin sees that.

He fucked with the wrong power couple.

The rest of our walk is brief and quiet, aside from the occasional car that drives by. The location Franklin sent us wasn't too far from Luciano's hideout, but we couldn't use one of his vehicles without risking Franklin realizing our alliance. And going back to our car seemed foolish, so here we are, hand in hand, strolling to another abandoned building in the industrial district.

We approach the clearing leading toward where we need to go, loose gravel crunching under our shoes, a train passing in the distance. My heartbeat is steady, my grip firmly on Johnny.

It's clear that our chances of survival are narrow, but I appreciate the fact that we get to do this together. It's totally bat-shit crazy, to have such a mindset—I'm well aware of that. There's something to be said about fully giving yourself to someone, though. Mind, body, and soul. Often, people find this very thing, but it's one-sided. It's rare when that connection goes both ways, but with it comes the ability to do anything for the person you love without reservation. Because at the end of the day, what's more important than that?

I sacrifice myself, because Johnny does, too.

A metal door creaks open up ahead, and a large man steps out into the night. His arms are crossed over his chest, and his face is solemn. He studies us each continued step of the way.

Johnny tenses slightly and glances down at me.

I can sense his hesitation. I'm sure he'd rather push me away, forbid me from going into that building, and handle this himself. I know the feeling all too well, given it's the exact thing running through my mind, too. There's no convincing either of us otherwise, and there's no point in trying.

For a split second, I replay a million possible scenarios through my head, but not of the outcome of tonight. Of Johnny's future.

I watch as he graduates from college, starts his photography business, decides to dabble in cinema and goes off to win some kind of award. He maintains a relationship with his father, and it builds over the years. Wrinkles appear on his face, the scars fading with time. He's smiling, he's free...and I'm there with him each step of the way. We bounce around the world, traveling and exploring, and he surprises me with a party when my first novel is published. His character never falters, and somehow, he grows kinder with age. At one point, I even catch a glimpse of us running our own coffee shop. A very Johnny and Claire thing to do.

The massive man at the door puts his hand up, signaling us to stop. "Arms out. Turn around." His voice is thick and coarse.

So much for the guns we had tucked away.

We comply, outstretching side by side.

He pats Johnny down first, pulling out the two pistols tucked into his waistband. He slides them across the ground where another nameless man picks them up. He flips Johnny around, checking his front, and once he's confident Johnny is clean, he moves his attention to me.

He starts at the top of my head, moving his way down, across my shoulders, along my arms, up under my armpits. He hesitates for a second too long, his grimy hands hovering over my tits. Before Johnny can react, because I know damn well he's about to, I thrust my elbow back and slam it into the guy's face. I probably shouldn't have, but I'd rather it be me than Johnny.

There's a crack, followed by a slur of curse words. I immediately go back into the arms-out position like nothing happened at all.

I flit my gaze over to Johnny, a look of shock and pride on his face. I stifle the grin on my own.

"You idiot," the other guy says. "You let a girl break your nose? Seriously?"

"Viktor, she fucking decked me."

Viktor? Why does that name sound so familiar?

With my back still turned, I have to guess what's happening. There's a mild sound of shuffling, and a grunt.

"Get in there, clean yourself up." The new guy tells the one I injured. His footsteps approach behind me. "Sorry about that. Gleb can get a little *handsy*, if you know what I mean." He sighs and goes to work patting me down, but not in the creepy way Gleb had done. "Can't have these." He pulls the pistols from around my waistband and tucks them into his own.

Well, we tried.

"Turn," the new guy says.

I glance at Johnny, his jaw tense for obvious reasons.

I take in the man's face. It's nothing special. Dark eyes. Dark hair. Cookie-cutter mob-looking guy. Forty-something, and probably wishing he'd gone to college instead of choosing this as a career path.

He taps around my ankles one last time and throws a thumb behind him toward the door Gleb disappeared into. "You're good to go."

Johnny and I meet each other's gaze, a silent exchange speaking volumes between us.

He winks at me, and with that subtle gesture, I prepare myself for any possible outcome.

Our hands find each other, almost like their magnets, locking us together.

We step through the threshold, a familiar stench tickling my nostrils—the same one from when I was taken. A chemical sort of smell—a mix of bleach and the remains of whatever was produced here years ago.

It takes my eyes a second to adjust, but when they do, I spot Rosie tied to a chair in the center of the room, Franklin standing at her side, that knife from the video call pressed to her neck.

I want to break into a sprint, rush over and free Rosie, but I can't. Not yet. Any sudden move could cause Franklin to react more irrationally than he already is.

"Well, well, well, what do we have here?" Franklin calls out to us. With his free hand, he motions us over.

A fresh set of goons come up behind us and shoves us forward.

Still hand in hand, gripping each other tightly, we make our way closer.

I try to scan the space, count the sets of eyes on us, but it's too much. There are too many of them, and every time I think I've finished tallying them up, someone else appears from the shadows.

Franklin was no fool; he came prepared.

Which if you think about it, is slightly hilarious. He's *that* damn afraid of Johnny that he brought an army to fight his war. Fucking coward.

Johnny attempts to position himself in front of me, but I make sure to stay by his side. He's already handled so much on his own, I refuse to let that happen anymore.

"Let her go," Johnny tells Franklin.

Franklin tilts his head to the side. "Now, what's the rush? We're only just getting started." He looks down at her and runs the flat of the blade across her cheek.

Rosie squirms under him but it's no use. She's tied in place with no chance of breaking free. Panic seeps out of her, which only fuels my rage.

The door we came through slams shut behind us, a row of men in black blocking the way. The room seems to shrink as a wall of men closes in around us. Franklin in the center, two guys at his back, and Rosie at his mercy.

Johnny gravitates toward me, or maybe me toward him, and either way, we inch together, as if we can somehow combine our strengths to find a way out. Our plan suddenly falls flat with the sheer magnitude of the effort Franklin is putting in to keep us confined. We stop within six feet of my best friend and the man threatening her.

I stare at her, pleading with her to understand how sorry I am, and that we will do everything in our power to get her out of this alive, even if it means sacrificing ourselves for her.

A man approaches Franklin, whispering something into his ear and retires to his spot in the line.

Franklin's eyebrows raise and he nods his head. "Interesting." He focuses on Johnny. "You actually listened. I have to say, I wasn't sure you'd actually come alone."

Johnny stiffens. "Who was I supposed to bring along? We did everything you asked. Let her go."

"You know…" Franklin circles Rosie slowly, the knife still in his grasp. "I'll never relate. This whole *good guy* act you put on." He stops, holding the tip toward us. "What's the point? It makes you weak. Vulnerable. Easily predictable. I mean, how simple was it for me to find you? All I had to do was locate her." He points at me. "And once I knew you had her, I just took this one." Franklin nudges Rosie. "It's like taking candy from a baby. What's the point? You're willing to *die* for these people? What's wrong with you?"

"You got what you wanted." Johnny grips my hand tightly. "Take me instead. Kill me instead of her."

Franklin strolls over to stand behind Rosie. "Oh Johnny, I don't want to kill you, not yet. I want to *torture* you. I want to make you pay for every little inconvenience you've caused me. I want you to beg me to stop. And when you do, I'm going to keep going." Franklin shakes his head. "You won't die tonight, boy. Not the way you think you will. This is only just the beginning of your end."

A different but similar man appears at Franklin's side, telling him something quietly.

Franklin sighs. "It appears our fun here will be cut short, as I have an urgent family matter to attend to." He nods to someone behind us. "Let's wrap this up and pick up where we left off later."

I watch in horror as he grabs Rosie by the hair, tilting her head back and pressing the blade of his knife to her throat. Everything speeds up and slows down all at once, the sudden realization that none of us are going to make it out of this alive.

And if that's the case, I am going to do everything in my power to make sure I take Franklin with us.

Franklin moves first, a twitch of his wrist.

I drop Johnny's hand, leaping away from him as my scream ripples through the air at the sight of blood on my best friend's neck.

Rosie's frantic gaze meets mine, and a loud bang echoes throughout the building. Chaos erupts, and with that, the execution has turned to a war.

JOHNNY – 23

Gunfire, smoke, bodies flailing and voices crying out.

I duck and squint through the mayhem, desperately searching for the most important person in my world.

My breath catches in my chest. Where the fuck could she be?

My vision blurs, and a person stumbles into me, nearly knocking me down.

Their body hits the concrete with a thud.

I ignore them and continue my search, moving in the direction my soul urges me. "Claire!" I call out.

She was right here. Right at my side. Literally connected to me. And in one flash, she was gone.

In a matter of seconds, dozens of scenarios play through my mind, none of which diminish the panic coursing through me. The idea of something happening to Claire unleashes a tidal wave of fear unlike anything I've ever known.

I will rip apart every single person in here if a single hair on her head is harmed.

I shuffle toward the chair bolted to the ground. The one

with Rosie attached to it. The one Claire had rushed toward after Franklin drew his blade across her best friend's neck.

My heart aches. All I wanted was to keep Claire safe. To save Rosie. To get Claire far, far away from this madness and give her the life she deserved.

The shape of her comes into my line of sight, relief washing over me. I'm not sure if my feet have ever moved as quickly as they do, dodging every person and flying debris that comes my way.

I skid to a stop beside her. "Claire, are you…" But other than the damage already on her face, there is nothing physically wrong with Claire, just the terror raging through her as she keeps her hand placed firmly against Rosie's bleeding neck.

She turns to me, a helpless look I've never seen on her before. "Johnny, help me."

I immediately go into action, reaching across and into the waistband of Claire's pants, pulling out the small, concealed knife that the man who patted her down missed. I drag it along the zip ties holding Rosie in place, one by one freeing her from her restraints.

She collapses forward, Claire and I both catching her. Rosie drags her hands to her own neck in an attempt to stop the bleeding.

"Here." I tug the fabric out of her mouth and pull it down over her throat, then motion for them to put pressure on the wound again.

I barely get it in place before the entire building flashes with light and a loud explosion bows my eardrums.

"Fuck!" I throw my body over Claire and Rosie the best I can, shielding them from the debris.

Splintered wood and concrete chunks are raining down, and I look down to see a severed hand skidding to a stop a few feet from us.

A large figure barrels toward us, and I raise my arm to throw the knife in their direction.

Josey throws his arms up. "Whoa, it's me." He drops to his knees beside Claire, ducking when gunfire goes off near us.

We are surrounded by absolute chaos, corralling us in the center of this battleground.

Josey reaches behind him, drawing two guns and holding them out. "Here." He nods to Rosie. "I'll take her."

Claire meets my gaze, then Rosie's. She doesn't want to let her friend go, but she needs medical attention if she's going to live through this. And considering Claire and I are both unfamiliar with this kind of thing, it makes sense to let someone more experienced take control.

"I'll keep her safe," Josey tells Claire. He extends his arm and blocks a body from barreling into us. "But we need to go, *now*."

I can sense Claire wavering, resisting putting her faith in someone other than herself—other than me. It's her call, but I hope like hell she makes the right one.

Whatever that may be.

"Okay," Claire mouths the word, her fingers still pressed against the half-assed bandage around Rosie's neck. "Rose, this is Josey." Claire grabs one of the guns, hands it to me, and takes the other. She pushes Josey's hands around Rosie's throat. "Do *not* let her die."

An automatic gun goes off in the distance, and people scream and cuss and do their best to avoid the crossfire.

Cries of agony ring out, bullets finding their targets.

"I won't." He turns to Rosie, pressing his hand against hers. "Keep pressure on that, you hear me?" Josey scoops Rosie into his arms with ease. He gives us one final look. "Stay safe." And with that, he's off.

Josey only takes a few large leaps when a man appears from a cloud of smoke, a knife raised over his head. Josey pivots, missing the guy's first attack, but he's not so lucky on his second. The blade lands in Josey's upper thigh, nearly dropping him to his knees.

From my crouched position, I aim the gun in my hand, not wanting to waste another second. I pull the trigger, ending the life of the guy who attacked Josey in one fell swoop.

Josey lets out a muffled grunt and, holding Rosie in just one of his arms, pulls the knife out of his leg with the other. He tosses it to the side and takes off running toward the closest exit, disappearing.

Claire steadies herself, drops the magazine from the gun in her possession, examines it quickly and shoves it back in. She inhales, her gaze meeting mine. "Are you ready?"

There was a fierceness about her before, but it's been replaced with something deeper, something darker, something unstoppable.

There are infinite reasons why I love this girl in front of me, and each day I'm surprised to see more added to the list. The fact that she's prepared to go, guns blazing, by my side, is more than I deserve, but only continues to make my heart swell for her.

"Let's end this." I stand as she does and push my back to hers.

Together, we pivot and scan the room, looking for the one person whose death will end this nightmare.

The swarm has seemed to die down, quite literally. Countless bodies litter the floor, bloodied and tangled together in a sea of death and destruction.

Luckily, it seems Franklin has become too concerned with his potential sudden death to continue his pursuit of us. My only hope is that he wasn't able to escape when he had the chance.

A loud crack sounds in my ears and smoke flits from the barrel of Claire's gun.

Her target falls to his knees, then drops over. A straight, clean shot to the temple.

My heart picks up its pace. What have I done? What kind of world have I brought Claire into? Why did I ever think this would end in anything other than disaster?

"Over there." Claire catches my attention, whipping her pistol toward the largest section of people left standing.

I squint until I see a familiar shape. And then another. And surprisingly, another.

Franklin. Luciano. Miller. Plus, a bunch of people gathered around them, firing their weapons haphazardly.

Two large men rush toward me and Claire, malice on their faces. They bare their teeth and draw their guns.

"Claire," I spit out while raising my firearm, popping off shot after shot, securing our temporary safety.

The reverberation shakes my wrists, but I refuse to let it steal my attention. The smell of gunpowder and death fills the air.

I dash over and snatch their weapons, tucking one into my pants. "Here." I toss the other to Claire, which she takes without a second thought.

A commotion flows from the throng in the corner, and Franklin and his goonies bolt from behind their cover and across the room. Luciano steadies his aim, taking out one of Franklin's guys.

But Franklin's men manage to eliminate three of Luciano's.

Rage, unlike anything I've ever seen, illuminates Luciano's stone-cold features. He lets out a battle cry and takes off after his brother, Miller and a couple of others in tow.

Without backup, they're clearly outnumbered, meaning only one thing.

Franklin is going to win.

I rush toward the chaos, Claire like a shadow behind me.

Maybe Franklin was right, maybe it's stupid to care for people the way I do, but I refuse to think the life he chooses is the one more worth living. I will not allow anyone else to die at his hands, not if I can help it.

He has to be stopped.

Another violent explosion ripples through the building, dropping me to the floor. Bits of concrete rain down all around, and I do what I can to use my body as armor to protect Claire from the wreckage.

"Are you okay?" I scream at her over top of the ringing in my ears.

She nods, her eyes squinted to block out the dust floating through the hazy air.

I allow my gaze to float through the crowd, ignoring the blood all around. I grip my gun, firing a bullet and somehow landing it in the chest of one of Franklin's men. Another unfortunate sacrifice in the grand scheme of things. These types of guys will not be reasoned with, not with Franklin still alive. There's too much loyalty, too much hatred in their eyes. And for what? A pretty penny?

I was like them once, blindly following that same sick and twisted excuse of a human. But the difference between me and them is that I never would have gone along with this. Not the kidnapping and torture of innocent people. The slaughter of many with no disregard because of some personal vendetta. Because I *outsmarted* him. How do they not realize the error of their ways? Of his ways? How is any of this justified?

One by one, Claire and I bolt across the dimly lit battlefield of a building to catch up to Luciano and Miller and the only other guy left on their side. The five of us run to duck behind a shipping container and catch our breaths.

Panting, Luciano grabs my shoulder. "You're alive."

"No shit. So are you." I flip my head toward where we came from. "What the fuck are we going to do? We're outnumbered."

Luciano runs his hand through his hair, sweeping it out of his sweat-soaked face. He drops the empty magazine from his gun and pulls another from his pocket. "I'm out after this." He dips his head toward a few bodies nearby, to their weapons at their sides.

Claire stares eagerly ahead, waiting for us to come to some kind of decision. Whatever it is, she'll be on board. She wipes her head on her shoulder, and her tongue traces the cut on her bottom lip.

Luciano sighs, glancing at the few faces left. He lowers his voice. "We'll have to charge them. I don't think he'll expect it."

Franklin calls out. "Brother, are you hiding from me?" He laughs, a sick and twisted sort of cackle. "Just like when we were children. Strange company you keep, though."

Luciano and I exchange glances.

Franklin is still unaware of our connection, the reason for our alliance. He has no idea the line he's crossed numerous times in Luciano's eyes.

"Luce, let's call a truce." Franklin giggles to himself. "That rhymed."

"He's getting closer," Miller whispers to us.

"Brother, I have a bit of unfinished business with your friend there," Franklin continues. "I'm all for answering to breaking the treaty and coming onto your territory, but can we do it another time? This doesn't have to be answered in bloodshed, not between us."

"He's not my friend," Luciano grits through his teeth, standing up and stepping out into the open.

The three of us dart after him, our weapons drawn with our fingers resting against the triggers.

The smell of burning flesh and the taste of metal reminds me of what's on the line. My head throbs and a lingering odor stings my eyes.

Franklin raises his gun, pointing it at the man standing between me and him. "Then, you wouldn't mind me…"

"He's my…"

Franklin doesn't wait for Luciano's response; he simply shoots. He doesn't care about anything, or anyone, other than the stupid fucking vendetta he has against me.

"Son." Luciano's word hangs in the balance as the bullet pierces his chest.

My mouth drops open, my heart clenching. I extend my arms, catching my father before he tumbles onto the disgusting floor. We collapse together—red instantly seeping through his shirt.

Another shot rings out, then another.

I glance up, complete shock rattling Franklin's features, his men dropping like flies beside him. Claire and Miller take them out one by one with Franklin's momentary distraction.

Claire glides around like she's floating, maneuvering herself strategically as if she was an elegant ice skater, but instead she's a ruthless assassin. Really, she's just an angry soul, hell-bent on getting the revenge she's been hungry for.

For once, I'm not worried about her, because I know damn well she can take care of herself. Who I fear for is the man in my lap, bleeding out at a rapid rate.

"Johnny," he mumbles.

I focus my attention on him, pushing on the leaking wound. "Shh."

Luciano stares at me, and it's like I'm looking in the mirror. "I didn't know," he tells me.

"What?"

Luciano coughs and winces. "I didn't know. About you. I would have been there if I knew."

And somehow, despite all of my doubts up until this moment, I believe him, because in a matter of a few days, he's proven more to me than I could have imagined.

"You're going to be okay." It's like my reassurance is more for me than it is for him. I only just got him in my life. I won't accept that he's gone this soon. Bad things keep happening but this, no...I won't accept it.

Red trickles from the corner of Luciano's lips. He wheezes, blood splattering out. "It didn't matter that I wasn't there..."

I shush him again but it's no use, he's determined to say his piece.

"You turned out exactly..." His lids become heavier as he forces himself to meet my gaze. "Exactly the man I would have hoped for."

"Johnny!" Claire's voice pulls my attention.

She's standing there, the barrel of the gun aimed at the man on his knees in front of her. Miller is within arm's length of her, there in case she needs him, but not overstepping.

Franklin. The man I have been tormented by for way too long. The man who ruins lives. Who will stop at nothing to hurt every single person in his path for no good reason other than to fill his twisted desires. Who shot his own flesh and blood, his brother, because he stood in his way.

Who will now die at the hands of the most beautiful angel I've ever seen.

My fallen angel, sweet and fearless in all her glory.

"It's up to you now." Luciano's voice is a choked murmur.

"Do it," I say through gritted teeth.

Franklin's eyes go wide, his hands rise further in the air, he opens his mouth to speak, but it's no use—we're not here to negotiate, not with him.

And with that final command, Claire pulls the trigger, blasting a bullet into the side of his head.

The shot rings out, a loud and thunderous echo in the largeness of the open space.

Franklin collapses with a thud onto the floor, ruby-red pooling around him.

Claire towers over him, firing off shot after shot into his

chest, blood splattering all over her body and face, until the magazine in her gun runs empty.

I allow myself to see it through her eyes. To feel the liberation through her.

This would be the perfect moment to sigh in relief. To relish in this bittersweet triumphant victory. But when my gaze cascades from her to the man dying in my arms, I find it a bit too difficult to celebrate.

CLAIRE - 24

Franklin is dead.

And I killed him.

I ended him, and honestly, the rush that consumes me is euphoric.

But it's also short-lived, considering the dozens of dead bodies surrounding us, and the dying man in Johnny's lap.

His father. Luciano Bane. Bleeding out and taking me uncomfortably back to the night of my birthday when Franklin ordered someone to shoot Johnny. I thought I had lost him then. The wound wouldn't stop oozing. The light in his eyes flickering until they closed for what I thought was the last time. If Johnny remotely feels anything like I did that night, I hate that for him.

I hate that he has to continue suffering at the hands of Franklin, even after I emptied countless rounds into his body.

It was probably excessive, but I had to be sure. Sure that Franklin had no chance of coming back from the dead and ruining Johnny's life any more than he already has.

I drop to my knees next to Johnny, helping him hold the weight of Luciano.

Miller drags his phone out of his pocket and pushes a few buttons, quickly putting it to his ear. "Immediate code eleven. I repeat, code eleven. Location incoming. We need all crews available." He scans the devastating contents of the building. "*All available crews.*" Miller disconnects the call and clicks the screen again. He kneels beside us and takes Luciano's hand in his, flipping it over and pressing his fingers to Luciano's wrist.

Luciano can't be dead. I won't permit my mind to wander in that direction. He has to be okay. For Johnny's sake. If I force my thoughts on him making it out of this alive, it will come true, right? Isn't that how manifestation works?

When I pictured Johnny's future earlier, Luciano was a part of it. He played an active role. Fluttering in and out, sharing laughs and successes and making up for the lost time. A positive role model in this otherwise negative world. A sliver of good coming from this terrible situation.

But as the blood continues to flow out and onto the ground, I worry that my premonition was a false hope. A reality that may never come to fruition. Sealing Johnny's fate to be alone in this world, but for me.

Except now he has Josey—a cousin he never knew existed. The two worked side by side in Franklin's organization and had no idea they were related.

And there's Bram—Johnny's found father. Now that Franklin is gone, we can return to see him once the dust settles.

Maybe Johnny can become Johnny again, just fade back into the person he really is, and put all the secrecy behind him. Behind us. We can go on and live our lives like the age-appropriate people we are.

Who am I kidding, though? This shit has changed us. And I'd be lying if I said we'd ever return to the people we were before this. I wouldn't want to, anyway. A darkness has taken hold and I embrace it for what it is.

Johnny's gaze trails over to mine, fear seeping out of him.

Our connection runs deep between us, giving us the ability to tune in directly to each other. It's one of the reasons we work so well—we can anticipate one another's needs.

This is something I'm not sure how to fix. I'm not a doctor. The only things I can handle are the occasional bumps and bruises Johnny stumbles home with, not a gunshot wound to the chest. I couldn't even help him when he was the one bleeding out in my arms.

Commotion draws my attention from the entryway. Countless people run inside the building, jogging in various directions. A trio approaches us and drags Luciano from Johnny. Two of them lift him onto a stretcher and the other cuts through Luciano's clothes.

I grab Johnny and turn him away from the sight of his father, near death.

The second Johnny's attention is away from him, he fully focuses on me. His gaze scans my frame, looking for any kind of injury.

I almost wish there was one so it would distract his mind from the more pressing situation—his dying father.

Kind of like how all of this has stolen my direct attention from freaking out about my best friend's slit throat.

I shove that thought away. I refuse to break down when Johnny needs me most.

Once Johnny realizes I'm completely free of any major damage, he reaches forward and pulls me to his chest. "Claire," he breathes. "Christ, you are brave." He says the words with equal parts admiration and annoyance. "Are you hurt?"

I shake my head against him and wrap my arms around his torso. "No."

Truthfully, I'm absolutely unscathed, aside from my prior wounds. The fact that Johnny and I are both alive, and Franklin is dead, feels like a miracle.

We did the fucking impossible.

We defeated Franklin.

Miller steps up to us. "They're taking him to Methodist Hospital. He has a room there, but it'll take a bit to get everything in order. I'll text you the details." He flits his finger at us. "I'd use the time to get cleaned up."

"What about…?" I wave my arm around us, halting my question when I notice the room is already tidier than it was.

Most of the bodies have been carried out. The weapons are piled into one general heap in the middle and cleaning supplies are stacked along the wall.

"Taken care of, ma'am."

Did Miller seriously just call me what I think he did?

Johnny goes stiff beside me.

I follow his gaze to the lifeless form that caused all of this destruction.

Franklin.

"You're sure he's…"

Miller and I both respond, "Yes."

Johnny seems to relax slightly, his body still rigid.

I take in a breath, steadying myself before I allow myself to speak. "Have you heard from Josey? Do you know if Rosie…"

Miller trains himself on me. "Josey would have taken her to the same hospital. Luciano has staff on call there. I haven't spoken directly to him, no. But if they're anywhere, it would be there."

Miller appears young, but he seems to have his shit together. He knows the ins and outs of Luciano's operation, and immediately stepped in when Luciano went down. If I didn't know any better, I'd say Miller was Luciano's right-hand man. But Miller is barely out of high school, that can't be true?

"Claire, Johnny." Miller looks to each of us, as if confirming that's our names. "You may have won your war, but this is only the beginning of what's to come. With Franklin gone, and Luciano hanging in the balance, it's only a matter of time until things erupt. The feud between these two has gone on for decades, a thick line drawn in the sand, with loyal men and women on both sides." Miller glances at the door where Luciano was carted out of. "If he makes it out of this, he's going to need your support."

A life I never wanted for Johnny: crime and danger. A world he has been desperately trying to escape since the moment he stepped foot into it. One that has nearly killed him on numerous occasions, and put countless others in harm's way—including me.

We thought ending Franklin meant we could finally be free of this chaos.

In reality, it was the start of something much bigger.

Because who am I kidding? We can't walk away now. Not after everything we've been through. If there are more out there like Franklin, there's no way Johnny will sleep soundly at night knowing he could have done something to stop them.

And there's no chance in hell that I'd forsake the man who has done more for me than anyone else. Who has proven time and time again that doing the right thing is, in fact, the right thing.

He'll have his doubts, but not because he doesn't think he should offer his assistance, but because he won't want to involve me. His main reason for ever shutting me out in the first place was to shield me from any danger, to protect me. What good did that do, though? We were drawn to each other in an uncontrollable way, even when we both tried to keep our distance.

Where Johnny goes, I go.

I would follow Johnny to the ends of this earth, and I confirm that when I look over at him, his beautiful green eyes staring down at me, and say, "You're stuck with me, remember?"

He stares at me, a sudden seriousness about him, like he realizes for the first time that I really am here to stay. No matter what, I am with him.

"*H*e's not answering," Johnny tells me from our closet. He throws a dark T-shirt over his head and pulls a top out for me.

I rush over, dragging it onto my clean body while letting out a muffled groan. Does this mean that Josey doesn't want to tell us the bad news over the phone? That Rosie didn't make it? Sure enough he'd find some way to let us know if she succumbed to her injuries.

Rosie was someone who never should have been involved. An innocent bystander that didn't deserve what came to her.

I sigh, realizing how Johnny must feel toward every single person who's been wrapped up in this nightmare.

I love Rosie like a sister, and that only compounds the rage inside of me. If there was some way to resurrect Franklin and end his life again, over and over, that still wouldn't be retribution for what he's done.

My only consolation is hoping whatever he faces in the afterlife is far more tortuous than what I'd prefer to do to him.

"Claire." Johnny plants his hands on my shoulders, steadying me and staring into my eyes.

Within a second, calm rushes over me. How does he have that kind of power over me?

"Josey probably doesn't have his phone. And I can't imagine he has my new number memorized. We're going, now. Okay?"

I study the way the green in his eyes swirls together with a golden amber. A dark fleck here and there. An even darker rim around the outside of them, nearly onyx, and contrasting beautifully against the emerald. His black lashes highlight them even more, giving a wonderful depth to his gaze.

My attention falls to that freckle I tried to scrub away many, many moons ago. The first night I saw just how vulnerable this man before me could be. I had no idea, but I was falling for him then. My heart had a mind of its own, tethering me to that beautiful soul of his. From the moment we quite literally bumped into each other, there was no escaping the magnetic pull that brought us together.

Life may have thrown us both some incredibly difficult curveballs, but it brought us to one another. We've fought like hell to be here, and we will continue fighting, because that's what you do when you find something this incredibly rare.

"Okay," I finally breathe.

We both have lives hanging in the balance, but at least we have each other to anchor us in place.

Johnny's phone buzzes, and he reaches for it without hesitation.

I look over his shoulder, the screen lighting up with details from Miller, the kid who isn't exactly a kid.

"You ready?" Johnny shoves the thing into his pocket and grabs the handle of the backpack containing a few essentials: phone chargers, clean clothes for Rosie, toothbrushes, change for the vending machine.

There's no telling how long we'll be there, and I'm sure Rosie will be anxious to get into something fresh that doesn't tie in the back. Although, if anyone can pull off a hospital gown, it's definitely her.

If she made it through Franklin's attack.

How will I even begin to explain to my best friend what happened to her? And how it was my fault? I've already been so fucking secretive about everything in an attempt to not get her involved, and here she is, near death because of it. Because of me.

It just goes to show that being open and honest with the people you care about is far better than keeping secrets. At least to those who could potentially be directly involved.

It'll be difficult, telling her the truth, but she deserves to know anything and everything she wants to help her make sense of the situation.

The drive to the hospital is short but somehow feels like an eternity.

Johnny grips my thigh in an attempt to settle both my and his own nerves. He glances over at me every now and then, like he's checking to make sure I haven't evaporated into thin air.

My jaw stays clenched, my mind wild at the possible outcomes we may find.

We've already lost so much, and it's likely that the losses keep coming.

We pull up to the place where Miller told us to park, and a man dressed in black greets us. Johnny goes rigid, but recalls the text he received, telling him that a guy would be waiting to take our car.

The man holds out his hand, waiting for the keys.

Johnny plops them into his palm and rushes around to get my door, but I'm already halfway out before he gets there.

I cannot stand being this close and not knowing if Rosie is dead or alive.

We've been friends almost our entire lives. Surely I would *know* if she was gone. There is an empty pit in my chest, but maybe it's from the worry, not the result of this unfortunate winter night.

Johnny weaves his fingers through mine and guides me up the few concrete steps leading into the back of the hospital. It's private, secure, and totally what I imagined given our *criminal* circumstances.

The sterile air hits me the second we walk through the threshold. Bright, fluorescent light shines down on a single hallway. I grip Johnny tighter, the uncertainty of things becoming increasingly dire. Within a matter of moments, I will know if Rosie made it out of this alive. And in a few hours, the fate of Luciano will follow.

We walk the path, each step closer causing my heart to beat that much harder.

The entry swings open, my eyes taking a second to adjust to the empty waiting room area. My gaze settles on the man I slapped, the man who carried my dying best friend away from me only a little while ago.

He stands, meeting my gaze, a sad but hopeful smile written on his hardened face. Josey nods, telling me everything I need to know.

Rosie—she's alive.

JOHNNY – 25

Waiting is the hardest part.

We've faced half the battle. Claire's best friend making it out of this with her life. But now, what will happen to Luciano? Will he survive, too? Is this what Claire felt like when she was stuck in a stupid hospital room, waiting for the outcome of my surgery?

Josey clasps my shoulder, forcing me to look at him. "He's a tough man, give him some credit."

"Yeah," I mumble.

It dawns on me that Josey knows this man who happens to be my father far better than I do. Luciano is practically a stranger to me—one that sacrificed himself by going into battle against Franklin to save my ass. He easily could have stayed out of it, not charged headfirst into that building, risking his life in the process. Sure, there was already a war between the two of them, but like Miller had said, it's been going on for decades; it could have easily waited for a few more.

His last words flutter through my mind—that he didn't know. That he wasn't aware I was ever created, let alone existed in the world. That he would have been there, had he known.

What would life have been like if I had an involved father? Would I have stayed out west? Gone east with him? Would I be like Josey or Miller? Would I be something similar to Luciano, or worse, like Franklin?

In a way, Luciano and I have things in common: our stubborn-headed need to do the right thing, and to help those that need help. The apple didn't fall too far from the tree on that one.

But why wasn't he aware? Why did my mom never tell him? She and I never spoke of the man who played a role in creating me, and honestly, I just assumed it was another one of the lowlife idiots she hung around. I never asked questions, because I wasn't totally sure she knew herself who my father might be.

And maybe she didn't.

Things could have been so different if she did, though.

I'd like to think that Claire and I would have crossed paths at some point, regardless of what path we were on in life. I mean, hell, she lives in the same town as my father now. Perhaps we would have stumbled into each other on the street out in front of the café, and I would have offered to buy her a cup of coffee. Then we'd laugh over bumping hands grabbing for the cinnamon shaker at the same time, and our love story would have begun there.

I would have found her, in any universe, in any lifetime.

And in each one, I'd know it was her with a simple look.

Even before we really knew each other, we were never strangers. There's always been this undeniable familiarity between us. Like our souls met long ago, and our bodies were only just catching up.

Claire is the part of me that I never knew was missing until she filled the void.

"Hey," she whispers softly. "Rosie is awake. Will you go back with me?"

There's this sadness about her that tells me she needs me; I can recognize it easily because it's the very thing I'm feeling, too. After everything we've been through, I don't want to be away from Claire either, not even for a second.

"Of course." I clasp her hand and follow behind the male nurse that came for us.

Rosie's room is right off the hallway of the waiting area, which is right next to the one Luciano will be in if he makes it through surgery. He's been in there for hours, and we still haven't heard one way or another if he will survive. I guess no news is better than bad news.

The twenty-something nurse holds open the door for us.

Claire tugs me along, rushing to Rosie's side. "Rose."

"Cla—," Rosie struggles to speak.

There's a bandage wrapped around her throat, and she looks like she could use a shower, but other than that, she's very much alive. And considering the alternatives, I'd say she's lucky. Franklin had no intentions of sparing her life, and had Luciano not stormed in when he did and started firing, she would have met the fate Franklin had decided for her.

"Shh, don't say anything." Claire drops my hand and smooths Rosie's blonde hair back from her forehead. "I'm so sorry."

The same words I've told Claire over and over for getting her involved in this twisted web of peril.

Rosie furrows her brows and tries to shake her head. She winces and pulls her hand to her neck. She sighs, clearly annoyed with not being capable of speaking freely.

"Truly, I never meant for you to get hurt." Claire lets out a breath of her own. "I'm so glad you're okay. That you're *going* to be okay."

Rosie's lips part, and despite her injury, she speaks anyway, "Are you?"

Claire glances over at me, and then at Rosie. "Yeah." She hesitates before continuing, "The man who did this to you…"

I place my palm on Claire's shoulder, a small gesture to let her know I'm here, that I'm always going to be here.

Claire straightens up, her jaw tensing slightly. "He's gone."

"Like, he escaped?" Rosie croaks.

"No, he's dead," I tell her before her panic sets in.

"I killed him," Claire confirms.

Rosie blinks a few times, soaking in what Claire just said.

Is she going to freak out? Is she going to be afraid of her best friend? Someone she's known her whole life is suddenly a killer standing before her. Will she be devastated by the news or will she understand, the same way I have for everything Claire has done? Every single brave and fearless choice she's made to take control of her life, to protect those that she loves.

In the time it takes Rosie to form a response, I can imagine the range of emotions Claire speeds through. It's the same I've experienced every time I've told her something that could threaten to break us apart. There's this terrifying uncertainty of how someone will react that makes time slow to a crawl.

"Good," Rosie finally sputters.

And like that, the tension in Claire's shoulders relaxes, a feeling I know all too well.

Acceptance. Understanding. Insecurities being thrown to the side.

Claire grips Rosie's hand. "I have so much I need to tell you, but it's late." Claire glances at the clock above Rosie's bed. "Get some rest. We'll talk in a few hours, okay?"

Rosie nods, her lids already heavy from the pain medication they have her on. We knew she wouldn't be awake long, but it was enough for Claire to get her little bit of peace from seeing her best friend open her eyes.

Claire and I start to make our way out of the room when Rosie speaks up.

"JJ..." She stares right at me.

"Yeah?"

"Thanks," Rosie tells me, her expression and tone speaking a million words despite having just said the one.

She is a part of Claire, and for that, I will do whatever it takes to save her, too, even if it means risking my own life.

"I can't believe you did it." Josey shakes his head. "You two are fucking crazy."

Claire lays her legs across me in an oversized chair in the waiting room of this hospital. She keeps dozing in and out while we wait to hear something from one of Luciano's doctors.

It's like we're stuck in this weird limbo of not being able to be happy he made it or start the grieving process if he didn't. The uncertainty is fucking killing me.

Even Miller's nerves are beginning to show. The dude is sitting at the opposite end of the room, making phone call after phone call and glancing at the main door every few seconds.

"You're perfect for each other, that's for sure," Josey adds. He holds his leg and repositions himself, groaning a little in the process.

I tighten my hand around Claire's calf, pulling her closer to my chest. Claire's face is bruised and swollen, her bottom lip busted, but somehow, she's the most beautiful human I've ever laid my sights on. I still can't believe I get the honor of calling her mine.

"How you holding up?" I ask him, eyeing the bandage wrapped around his thigh.

He shrugs like it's no big deal. "Meh. I'll be fine."

"You took a flying knife to the leg, dude."

"I did, didn't I?" Josey chuckles. "Thanks, by the way, for saving my ass when it happened."

"Of course, man."

Josey sighs and leans back. "I never did care for him. Guy was always a dick."

"You're telling me," I laugh.

His tone shifts to serious again. "Franklin. Dead. Never thought I'd see the day. I'm relieved. Honestly." Josey lifts his shoulder. "A little terrified of what's to come, though."

I flit my gaze across the room at Miller, recalling what he had said about what would happen now that Franklin is gone, and Luciano is in limbo. Hearing it from Josey makes it that much more real.

Solving my one problem may have created a fuckload of others.

And that alone makes me feel guilty as hell.

What if Luciano doesn't make it out of this? What will that mean for his organization and for everyone that works for him? Will they be overthrown by Franklin's minions? Who will take over for either of them? Franklin had a wife; she was there when I petitioned to take Billy's place, and she was the only reason Franklin decided to take me on. Will she take on his responsibilities? And if she does, what will she think when she finds out I was the reason why her husband was killed? What will happen to Josey? Will he go home, or will he stay here? Why was he ever involved with Franklin to begin with?

"Josey," I say when the question strikes me. "The fuck were you doing working for Franklin anyway?"

Josey leans forward and exhales. "It's a long, very fucked-up story. Family obligations and shit. Ended up biting off more than I could chew, kind of got stuck there with him. But..." Josey rakes his hand across his beard. "Now that my Gram is on her deathbed, it kind of changes things."

Grandma? Oh right, he mentioned that's why he was out here. Does that mean...?

Josey shakes his head. "On my dad's side, not my mom's. By

the way, my mom was your aunt, if you're wondering how we're cousins. Franklin, Luciano, and Cecilia were siblings."

His use of the word *'was'* and *'were'* coming through loud and clear. Past tense.

Josey must notice the way my expression changes because he continues. "Now it's just Luciano."

If he manages to live past the gunshot wound to his chest.

Miller stands from his spot and comes over. "Sorry to interrupt, but Josey, if you have a minute?"

Josey stays in place. "Yeah, sure, man, what's up?"

Miller glances over at me and Claire and then at Josey.

"They're family, anything you have to say to me, you can say it to them." Josey slaps me on the shoulder and winks.

"Very well." Miller clears his throat. "Who's left in charge on the West Coast?"

Josey scratches his temple. "Dominic, probably."

"Who's directly under Dominic?"

"Um...let me think. Cohen, Magnus, possibly Simon."

"Do you know if Franklin delayed any shipments while he was away, or if he carried on with business as usual?" Miller takes notes on his phone.

"He was dealing with some shit from up north. I overheard it before I left. Not sure if he squared it away or not. I can't imagine he would have slowed down for this. He probably thought he'd be in and out in a few days."

"Think you could give me a list of his known suppliers?" Miller stares at Josey.

It's such a strange sight. The two of them couldn't be any more different. Josey clearly has over ten years on him, plus at least eighty pounds. Josey is a large man, big-ass muscles, intimidating as hell. And there's Miller, this freckle-faced kid who doesn't look like he should be running numbers or making the arrangements for a café, let alone a criminal underground. Miller has basically taken over Luciano's operation since he's been incapacitated, and if Luciano makes it out of this alive, I'm going to suggest that he give Miller a raise. I don't know what this kid makes, but it's probably not enough for the work he's done. And if anything, I could stand to learn a thing or two from him, especially if I'm going to be living in this kind of world permanently.

"What can I do to help?" I ask him.

At this, he seems stunned. "You want to help?"

"Yeah." I point toward the motionless door. "This waiting game sucks. If there's something you need me to do, just tell me."

Miller juts up his lip, his brows raised with surprise. "Cool. Thanks." His expression has him looking totally his age.

"I do have to ask though, how old are you?"

Miller rolls his eyes. "I'm twenty-one."

Now it's my turn to be shocked. "Holy shit, no way."

He folds his arms across his chest. "Come on, get it out. I know. I know."

Here I thought the kid was maybe still in high school, and it turns out he's older than I am.

"You must have good genes," Claire chimes in.

The latest talk seemed to wake her up a bit from her dozing in and out.

My heart nearly lurches out of my chest when the door we've stared at for hours now opens. A stern-faced man with gray hair walks through, a clipboard clutched in his grasp.

I desperately try to read his face. To determine what he's going to say before he says it, in some pathetic attempt to brace myself for whatever the outcome is.

On one hand, I could be fatherless. The man I only just met could be dead as a result of a bullet from his own brother. I've gone my entire life thinking my dad wanted nothing to do with me or my mother, I guess having him in my life for a few days is better than nothing. He'll be dead but I'll know that I was wanted—that he didn't abandon me, and that he was a decent man.

On the other hand, he could very well be alive. My dad could be living, breathing, and still potentially capable of being in my life. There's so much left that we've yet to do. Endless firsts between a father and a son—things I never got to do with him because of our weird circumstances. There's still time to make up for all of the lost years between us. To take back what was robbed from us.

I hold my breath and wait for something, anything to rid me of this hell I've been locked in.

The doctor glances anxiously at each of us, like he's not sure which person to focus on for this news. "Mr. Bane did not make it through surgery."

He's *dead*? I must not have heard him correctly. Maybe the excessive gunfire and explosions fucked with my ability to hear, not to mention my pounding heartbeat thudding loudly in my ears.

I jump out of my seat, Claire joining me at my side. Josey and Miller stand huddled around this newcomer who wields more information than we do.

"He's dead?" Miller asks the question all of us have on our minds.

The doctor nods, a formal sadness on his face. "I'm sorry."

A collective silence fills the room.

"The bullet damaged his ribs and nicked his lung. We were able to remove it and repair what we could, but the damage was too extensive. We couldn't get the bleeding under control." He shifts his glance around again, still uncertain who he should be speaking directly to.

He continues to say words, but it all becomes a blur.

I reach to grab onto Claire's hand, allowing her touch to calm my aching heart. I didn't realize how incredibly scared I was to lose this man. I thought there was hope. I was sure that he would make it through this. That one day, this would fade into our past. But that's not how the world works. No, time and time again, it reassures me that bad things happen to good people.

My chest tightens, strings pulling and tearing at a loss so fresh. It was one thing when I thought he didn't want to be a part of my life, to think he didn't care. But to know he did, and to lose him, it hurts worse than I could have imagined. Tears well in my eyes but I force them away. I will not break. Not here. Not now. Not like this.

It can't be possible, but it is.

He's dead.

My dad is dead.

CLAIRE – 26

*L*uciano is dead, and Rosie is alive.

I'd be lying if I said I didn't believe like hell that we'd all somehow make it through this unscathed. But the universe was not on our side, reminding me that only so many miracles are allowed to happen in such a short time.

Franklin is gone, no longer a threat to our safety. But our loss was massive. Not to mention, we unleashed a whole new world of danger into our lives. It might not be immediate, or lurking around every corner, but we are fully consumed in a world we thought we were going to escape from.

If it's the price I have to pay to be in Johnny's life, I will gladly go running into the fire to stay with him.

If someone would have pulled me aside a year ago and told me that this is how things would play out, I'd never have believed them. I knew things were going to change, that I was going to get away from Griffin, but I didn't think it would happen *this* way. I never would have guessed I'd become *this* version of me. The Claire that was always there, just under the surface, waiting for me to realize and unleash her.

This "face whatever comes her way and fights for what's right" kind of woman.

One that would manipulate and poison and shoot those in her path to save the ones she loves.

It's dark, darker than I imagined I could be, but it's me. And honestly, I don't regret any of it, because it got me to where I am today. If anything, I embrace it.

I glance across the room, my sights settling on Johnny, Josey and Miller at his sides. They're talking strategy on how to overcome the shit storm that is heading our way.

Within moments of finding out Luciano's fate, Miller went straight into executive mode, pushing aside his emotions and focusing on the task at hand. Johnny mirrored his hardened exterior and followed suit, and for the last few hours, they've been huddled in the corner of this dank hospital waiting area, discussing some kind of plan.

Worry courses through me at seeing Johnny put up such a cold front, but I don't take it personally. He's around other people, and I'm confident he doesn't want to appear vulnerable in front of them. The soft version of Johnny is reserved for me, and once we're outside of these walls, behind the privacy of our own, Johnny will feel safe enough with me to let his guard down.

People grieve in different ways, and I have to accept that for now, this is Johnny's.

My role is to harden myself into his rock, anchoring Johnny from spinning out of control.

Rosie sits in the chair across from me, the bandage still wrapped around her throat, but with the doctor's approval that she can get up and walk around a little. As soon as she got the go-ahead, she hopped into the shower in her attached bathroom and changed into the spare clothes I had brought her. They're not her style, but they're comfortable and clean. She was grateful to get out of that hospital gown, just like I imagined she would be.

"I can't believe you didn't bring me any makeup." Rosie cups her hand toward me and lowers her voice. "You didn't tell me how *cute* JJ's friend was."

"I told you on FaceTime, remember?" I glance over at Josey. "He's too old for you."

Plus, he is sort of a criminal. But aren't we all, if you really think about it? Mainly, it's the age difference. He's way more experienced, in every imaginable way, than Rosie. I don't want her to get hurt if she doesn't know what she's getting involved with. I've only been around Josey on a few occasions, I don't know him well enough to give my stamp of approval.

He did get her to safety and maybe saved her life. I guess he gets brownie points for that. And he gave Johnny insider information on that package situation. Okay, a few more points.

Rosie tilts her head to the side and deadpans. "Is not."

Somehow, no makeup, freshly tortured, she still looks like a supermodel.

Josey glances over his shoulder like he suspects he's being talked about. He winks at Rosie, turning around and focusing back on the boys.

Rosie blushes and starts to speak but ends up wincing, being completely taken out of the moment.

It feels wrong to even consider anything cheerful given the magnitude of the situation.

I shake my head back and forth. "Nope. Not happening. See, you're already getting hurt."

But if I know the power of love, if those two are meant to get together, there's nothing any of us could do to stop it from happening.

I settle my gaze on my own dark prince, the one I tried like hell to stay away from.

He runs his hand through his stubbly hair, growing irritated with himself at the lack of length.

"At least you can grow it out now," I whisper to him from across the room.

He probably can't hear me, but I tell him anyway.

Johnny pivots his head and looks right at me. He puckers his lips, blowing me a soft kiss and going back to the conversation.

Despite the heavy dark cloud over him at losing his father, there's a sort of lightness about him that hasn't been there before. A weight that was lifted from his shoulders. The burden of doing everything on his own is now replaced by the ability to count on others.

When I met him, he was alone. Relying on himself and no one else. He had Bram, but he kept him further than an arm's length. He didn't tell Bram the many struggles he faced, just handled them all on his own.

Since knowing Johnny, I've done my best to take some of that burden from him. To help him even when it's hard for him to let go. To show him that *sometimes* people can be trusted.

Johnny Jones is not a good man. He's a damn great one, and he deserves the same benevolence he puts out into the world. His soul is pure, and he is easily the most selfless person I've ever known. I am forever grateful that our paths crossed, and that I get to be his partner in this life.

He supports my hopes and dreams, empowers me to be a better woman. He is gentle and compassionate, intelligent and hilarious, not to mention, drop-dead fucking gorgeous. Most of all, he is the type of human I aspire to be. That everyone should want to be. He may be good at fooling people into thinking he's a bad guy, but his heart is big and when he loves someone, he gives it his all. And he will stop at nothing to make sure they're safe.

Even if he has to push them away. Even if he has to sacrifice himself for their wellbeing.

I let out a breath, allowing this new chapter to wash over me.

"So, what's next?" Rosie asks me, her expression solemn.

I take a look at the man who holds my heart, and the unlikely friends and family surrounding him.

Johnny holds out his hand, inviting me over to him.

It was only a matter of time before I was drawn back to him.

I grab Rosie's on the way, leading her out of her chair and over to sit with the guys.

Josey seems to gravitate toward her, cutting Miller off and sort of pushing him out of the way.

Miller rolls his eyes and moves to the other side.

Johnny meets my gaze. "We're coming up with a plan."

A memory of a scene incredibly similar flickers into my head: Johnny in the hospital, figuring out his move against Franklin. He may be dead, but his ghost still haunts us.

I repeat the words Bram had said that day, fully meaning them. "What can I do?"

Miller clears his throat. "Well, with the way things are, and everything kind of up in the air, I need to pull myself from the café full time. Which leaves it pretty much unattended." He gives Johnny a glance before settling on me. "I heard you had some experience in such."

"Waitressing maybe," I laugh unenthusiastically.

He isn't implying what I think he is, is he?

Johnny slides his hand over, resting it on top of mine. A silent but powerful gesture.

"It would be great if you could take over. You'll be trained on the operations, but you have some pretty solid references." Miller looks at me with a hopeful stare. "It's your choice, obviously, feel free to think it over."

I mill it around in my mind, coming to the same conclusion every single time.

"Okay, I'm in."

Miller's brows raise, a hint of surprise in his voice. "You are?"

I squeeze Johnny's hand. "Without a doubt."

"Great." Miller lets out a breath. "We can begin tomorrow, if that works for you."

I'll have to figure out how to factor in school, but now, without the pressing threat of hiding from Franklin, it should be simple finding a balance between everything. It's not like I haven't already done crazier things. The best part of all is that I get to do it with these people surrounding me.

"Yeah, tomorrow," I tell Miller.

Johnny nudges me to him, wrapping his arms around me from behind. He whispers into my ear, "I love you."

I weave my fingers around his, pulling him tighter. I tilt my head up to him.

He brings his lips down to gently rest on mine in a brief, but completely heart-melting moment of bliss.

"Get a rooooom," Josey calls out.

Johnny shoots him a death glare. "You're just jealous you're alone."

Josey narrows his gaze. "Am not."

"You two sound like children," Miller adds.

Josey and Johnny both turn to Miller.

"*Sound*, maybe, but you *look* fourteen." Josey nudges Miller teasingly in the shoulder.

And so it begins, the comradery between these three. An improbable bond that will form because of circumstances I never saw coming.

Rosie remains quiet, as if watching our situation play out as an outsider.

"I'd like to ask something." I shift my gaze between them.

Miller perks up his brows, clearly the de facto one in charge here. "By all means."

"Given my new position, am I allowed to hire anyone?"

Miller blinks at me, allowing the question to soak in. "Well, they'll have to be vetted, considering our unique situation. I could imagine you would need the help. So, yes. Yes, you can."

"What about Rosie?" I point to her, totally putting her on the spot but not caring.

She's my best friend, the one person other than Johnny I trust completely. I don't see anyone more perfect for the position than her. I'm not sure if she's even willing, but she's mentioned to me before about finding a side-gig, making this an opportune prospect for both of us.

"She has my full support," Johnny confirms.

My heart swells with joy at having my two favorite people get along so well.

"And what are your thoughts about this?" Miller asks Rosie.

She glances at me briefly and focuses on him. "I—I'd love to help, whatever way I can."

"Okay," is all Miller says in response. A simple word, confirming so much.

I wasn't confident either of them would be on board, but I had to at least try. Rosie is my own right-hand woman, and to have her at my side during this huge transition, it would be monumental.

Josey grips Rosie's shoulder, "Welcome to the team."

She glances up at him, careful not to tilt her head too much, and smiles. "Thanks."

I think back to the three of us out west in that hospital room—me, Johnny, and Bram—and how none of us would have ever imagined *this* would have resulted from our half-assed plan to fake Johnny's death.

But the thing about fate is you never really know where it will take you until you're there.

Because never in my wildest dreams would I have imagined bumping into a boy on my first day in a new town would lead me here.

My phone buzzes from its spot on the armrest of the chair across the room.

Johnny steps back, giving me space to get up, a mixture of concern and confusion on his face. Things couldn't possibly get any worse, right?

Maybe it's a telemarketer, trying to sell me some extended car insurance.

The contact on the screen sets my heart racing.

I glance back at Johnny, hoping that looking at him will somehow erase the panic now racing through me.

There was only one other thing left in limbo, threatening to ruin us.

The lethal dose of poison I used on Griffin.

The whole room goes silent, as if sensing the new danger.

I swallow the lump in my throat, click the green button, and drag the receiver to my ear. "Hello."

"Miss Cooper. This is Officer Donovan. How are you?" His usual formalities.

I force myself not to stammer. "I'm fine. You?" I keep my eyes trained on Johnny's.

"I'm well." His tone immediately shifts. "Listen, I don't want to take up any more of your time than I already have, but I wanted to call and let you know."

Oh God, this is it. He's going to warn me that the authorities are on their way. Or that they're starting an investigation based on the chemical they found dancing around Griffin's bloodstream. That it wasn't *complications*, but yet something much crazier that happened. That Griffin didn't die from an accident, that he was murdered.

I force the thought of being taken from this group of people before me away.

Even if the eye drops showed up, surely what's left of Luciano's organization is powerful enough to help me make this go away.

But that would be wrong. I killed Griffin. And I deserve to face the consequences that come from taking his life into my own hands. I've already shed enough blood.

"It appears I was correct in my preliminary assessment." A bit of static comes through Donovan's end. "Griffin Thomas died as a result of his injuries. His heart gave out."

His heart. The thing that the poison impacts. It causes a decreased heart rate and lowers the pressure, eventually killing a person if the dose is large enough and it goes untreated.

I did, in fact, kill Griffin. It just went completely undetected, like I had planned all along.

"Anyway, I know this experience has been traumatic, and I do regret that I was unable to get the justice that you and many others deserved."

Little does he know I got it for all of us.

"Miss Cooper, are you still there?"

I blink, throwing myself back into reality. "Yes, sorry."

"No worries. I understand this is a shock. If there's anything I can do, feel free to reach out."

"Of course. Thank you."

"Take care, Miss Cooper."

"You, too."

And with that, the line disconnects, severing the last major uncertainty in my life.

Johnny makes his way to me within a second, his hands gripping my face. "What did he say?"

I should have thought to put it on speakerphone, but then I'd have to explain the entire situation, and I think my best friend has had enough of me being a murderer for one day.

"It was complications. He died from complications."

A new wave of relief crashes over me.

Ever since Donovan told me there would be an autopsy, I feared that I would be found out. That the poison would be uncovered, and that eventually, they would trace it back to me.

It wasn't getting in trouble that scared me, it was the thought of losing Johnny. The idea that my actions would be unforgivable and that they would take me away from him permanently.

But now, with the confirmation that they went undetected, I realize nothing is standing between us. We defied the odds stacked against us, overcoming things that threatened to break us apart. Time after time, we have been thrown into impossible situations, and somehow, we fought through the darkness and found the light. We never gave up, even when our backs were against the wall.

Only proving that no matter what, we will make it through, and we will do so together.

We are stronger as a team, as one.

"You had me worried there for a second." Johnny runs his thumbs gently along my cheeks. "I thought I was going to lose you, too."

A smile breaks across my beaten face, and despite my heart breaking for this tortured man in front of me, I remind him that I'm here to stay. "You're stuck with me, remember?"

EPILOGUE – JOHNNY

I flinch when a knock rattles the front door to our apartment.

Claire stops writing in her notebook and glances toward it. She's in a mad dash to get caught up on her college assignments if she wants to pass this semester. It wouldn't be the first time she's pulled off that kind of miracle, leaving me with no doubts she'll do it this time, too.

It's only been a week since the war with Franklin, but we're both clearly still on edge. The intensity of the situation hasn't worn off, and despite the immediate threat being eliminated, there's that lingering worry that remains.

"I'll get it," I tell her as I stand and make my way over toward it.

Glancing through the peephole, I catch Miller flipping his head both ways, eyeing the hallway while he anxiously waits for me to answer. A short man in a business suit at his side, a binder in his hands, a pair of black-rimmed glasses on his face.

I open the door, shifting my focus between them. "What's this about?"

"Mr. Jones." The guy holds his hand out toward me. "Bruce Green."

I hesitate, not really sure what the hell is going on.

"I'm here on behalf of Mr. Bane's estate management team."

I finally take Bruce's palm into mine and give it a firm shake. "Oh, right. Come on in."

Claire jumps up from her spot on the couch and moves toward the kitchen. "Can I get you anything to drink?"

Bruce shakes his head. "No, I won't be long, thank you."

Claire continues on her task anyway, grabbing four glasses and filling them with water. She carries them over and sets them down in front of each of us at the table. "Just in case."

"Thanks," Bruce says politely.

"You hungry?" she asks Miller, who in the short amount of time we've known him has become like a sibling to us.

Another addition to our strange found family.

"Maybe in a little bit," he tells her.

Claire settles into the seat beside me, sliding her fingers around mine in a subtle but powerful gesture. She knows how much I hate uncertainty, and this situation is bursting with it.

Bruce carefully unclips the tie around his binder, flipping it open and skimming the edge until he settles on a blue tab. "Mr. Jones." His gaze skims the page. "As the beneficiary for one Luciano Bane, you are entitled to the majority of Mr. Bane's assets."

My heart skips a beat and then thuds loudly. Did I just hear him correctly?

Beneficiary? Assets?

I swallow the lump rising in my throat.

My mouth drops open, but I find myself unable to speak.

"I'll provide you with a list to encompass the entirety of your inheritance, including, but not limited to, Bane's Café, the penthouse on Water Street, Front Street, and Walnut Avenue, Loose Change Laundry, and numerous other enterprises. You will also be taking over his..." Bruce stops to turn his attention toward me, lowering his glasses to get a better look. "Less official ventures."

This can't be true. I must have died back in that warehouse and this is some weird afterlife.

"Mr. Bane gave specific instructions that one Samuel Miller would be staying on with a salaried position to be your..." He runs his finger down the page to find the exact wordage. "Advisor." Bruce pauses. "Miller was also given a piece of real estate, a vehicle from Mr. Bane's collection, and a sum of cash."

Miller and I lock eyes briefly.

"Josey did, too," Miller adds. "He's part of your advisory board." He glances toward the door. "He should be here soon, actually, he just had to pick Rosie up first."

"Miss Claire Cooper?" Bruce turns to Claire, snapping me out of my stupor at the mention of her name.

"Yes," she confirms with a bit of a question mark in her tone.

"Mr. Bane left you money, too, with the instruction to use it for your tuition, and then the rest at your own discretion." Bruce flits his gaze at me. "And gave you co-ownership of Bane's Café, with Mr. Jones."

Claire releases my hand and points to the page he's getting his information from. "That must be some mistake." She shakes her head. "I don't need anything. That's..."

Bruce puts his palm in the air to stop her. "I don't determine these affairs, and I'm unable to make changes to them. I'm just the guy who gets to divvy them out. What you choose to do with them is up to you, but I must respect Mr. Bane's wishes and follow through with his estate plan."

Claire and I share the same thought process.

I did nothing to deserve any of this. I only knew this man a week, and he left basically his entire fortune to me? There had to be someone else in his life that this could have gone to. Hell, he and Miller had a better relationship than we did, why didn't he get all of Luciano's stuff? I was practically a stranger that shared the same DNA.

Luciano's final words cross into my mind. There was such sadness in his eyes when he told me he didn't know. That he would have been there if he did. Maybe this was his way of making sure I knew that he meant those words. That regardless of when our paths intersected, he would always be looking out for me.

I tilt my head toward Claire, disbelief wrecking both of our features.

The bruising on her face has nearly faded into a pale green that is easily covered up by a little bit of makeup. The cut on her lip has scabbed over, and will more than likely leave a lasting scar, a forever reminder of the day she was almost taken from me. Her brow and cheek have healed nicely, and with some extra care, may continue until they're good as new. The only remnants of them being the brutal memory that will never leave me.

But with every mark on both of us, the realization that we made it through, that despite everything that's happened, we're still here today.

Together.

Six months have passed since Luciano left us, and finally, Claire and I get the chance to do something we've been dying to do the second we broke free from Franklin.

I pull our black Audi into a parking spot across the street from our destination and hop out to open Claire's door. I scan the vicinity, disallowing any negative feelings to come rushing in at being near a place that caused so much trauma.

"My lady," I tell her.

"Why, thank you," Claire beams back.

We hold each other's hands tightly, the sun cascading down on our skin.

It's much hotter than I remember, especially after spending the winter out east. Now, it's the dead of summer, and the sun is making damn sure we're aware of it.

I reach toward the handle, gripping it firmly and grinning at Claire.

The bell on the door does that familiar dinging I've heard a million times before.

I breathe in the scent of home—a mixture of coffee and freshly baked muffins. A smell that could never be replicated, that is reserved for one place and one place alone.

"Sit wherever you want," a waitress tells us from a few tables down. She goes to work dumping the remaining plates into her plastic dishpan.

Claire makes her way straight to the counter, disregarding the odd looks she gets from a couple in a booth, and flips up the partition to step behind it. She holds it for me and I slide in after her.

Just then, the door to the kitchen swings open, a tall, gray-haired man appearing in front of us.

A mixture of shock, surprise, and then complete joy washes over him and into me.

His mouth drops open, and he reaches his arms out to envelop us both.

"Bram," I sigh.

He sniffles and continues to hug us tightly, despite the scene we must be causing.

"Johnny, Claire." Bram finally lets go. A bit of concern flits across his face. "Is everything okay?"

"Yeah," I breathe.

I'd be lying if I said life was easy, because taking over numerous businesses, properties, employees, and essentially stepping into the expensive wingtips of the powerful Luciano

Bane has been a huge fucking challenge, but along with it, a sense of security to go with that risk.

And I mean literally, I have a security detail now that pretty much shadows my every move. Claire has one, too, as does Josey and Miller and even Rosie. Basically, every vital member of Luciano's legacy. The wrath of Franklin didn't stop when he did, because his death caused a series of events to take place, throwing his entire organization into utter chaos and sending various threats our way. For the most part, it's been stabilized, at least enough that we could finally break away and visit someone who played such a huge role in shaping me into the man I am today.

"Here." Bram reaches for the nearby pot of coffee. He points toward the booth in the corner, the one me and Claire pretty much claimed as our own during our time here. "Go sit." He shoves us back through the way we came and motions for the waitress who greeted us. "Three cups, a shaker of cinnamon, and a half dozen blueberry old-fashioneds."

Claire and I slide in next to each other, our backs against the wall so we can scope out the diner, a habit that has only continued to intensify with each passing day.

Bram joins us a second later, the petite waitress on his heels.

He waits for her to finish setting the mugs on the table to speak. Bram sighs. "I can't believe it."

Claire puts a dash of cinnamon in my coffee and hers, and stirs them both. She nudges the one toward me and looks at the bright-eyed man across from her. "We missed you, Bram."

"The feeling is mutual." He fidgets with his spoon. "I was so damn worried about you two." His serious gaze cuts right through me.

I fucking hated leaving him the way I did. He had done so much for me, and I thanked him by disappearing into thin air, barely holding onto my life. I can only imagine the endless possibilities that ran through his mind and the countless times he must have thought the worst had happened.

I became a ghost, one that was hiding from a man that tried to kill me. I had given Bram close to nothing to hang on to, other than the weak possibility that if I was ever able, I would reach out to let him know I was okay. I couldn't risk contacting him after I had left, because there was no telling the lengths Franklin had gone through to keep tabs on me. I needed Franklin to assume that all Bram was to me was the dude who owned the coffee shop I liked to frequent. If he knew anything else, he would use it against me, just like he did with Claire, and with Rosie.

I couldn't protect Bram from two thousand miles away, so I did what I had to do to keep him in the dark. The less he knew, the better.

I reach across the table, resting my hand on his and forcing his gaze. "I'm sorry."

Bram's eyes glisten and he lets out a breath of air. "You have nothing to apologize for. I understand."

A father's love is unconditional, and I may have lost the man who brought me into this world, but the man sitting in front of me is more of a dad than I ever deserved.

The waitress sets a plate full of donuts on the table, pulling us out of our bittersweet moment. "Can I get you anything else?" She seems to notice all too late that she interrupted something. "Or I can come back?"

Bram wipes at his eye and forces a smile. "What do you say? You two kids hungry?"

Claire sets down her cup. "I could go for a stack of blue and a side of B."

Bram points his finger at me. "How about you?"

"Sure," I grin. "For old times' sake."

"Three orders, please," Bram tells the girl.

I take a long sip of my coffee, savoring the perfect combo of bitter and bold with a hint of spice. "Still the best cup of joe around."

And it's the truth. Even being a part-owner of a café, our roast will never compare. There's just something about being at home that makes things that much better.

"One more stop, then we can get going," I tell Claire.

Our time out west is drawing to a close. We only had a limited window, but we had to make the most of it. Visiting Bram was a given, something that was well overdue, but the last thing I have planned is a bit of a secret.

"We're going to miss our flight," Claire whines.

I tilt my head at her. "It's a private jet, it can wait."

Claire scratches at the blindfold around her eyes, and for a second, I think she's trying to look.

"No peeking," I remind her as I pull over and park our car.

I jump out and open her door, grabbing her hand and guiding her blindly out. I punch the code into the gate, watching the light illuminate green, granting us entry.

"Um, was that what I think it was?"

Can't get anything past Claire.

"Maybe, maybe not."

I take in a breath, glancing around to make sure everything is in place. String lights float like stars across the courtyard, dozens of candles illuminate the darkness, and flower petals gild the paved ground we stand on.

"Claire." I gently remove her blindfold and pat down her hair.

My heart thuds with anxious energy. The choice I'm about to give her—the one that could make or break everything.

Claire blinks to adjust her vision, taking in the spectacle I've made. She brings her hand to her chest. "Johnny."

"It was right here"—I point to the spot we're standing—"when I saw you for the first time. One of the darkest periods of my life, and an angel literally dropped right in my path. My soul knew before I did that you would be the person to guide me through. I was stubborn, stupid, and I tried like hell to push you away. To protect you. But the universe had a different plan. It was over there"—I point to the picnic table at the far end—"that I got the privilege to spend time with you, to get to know you, to see what a brilliant and wonderful person you are."

"J…"

"It was there"—I point to the rooftop access that no one uses—"that I shared with you pieces of me that I had never shared with another. I was so scared of losing you, but I knew I had to give you the option to walk away, that you deserved to decide for yourself." I let out a small chuckle. "You accepted me without question, which led to the most insane first kiss ever."

Claire blushes, and I run my hand through my hair. It's getting longer.

"This building is home to some of the best and worst memories. But without them, Claire, it wouldn't have brought us here, to this one. And maybe that path was a little jagged, but I am eternally grateful for whatever force brought us together." I drop down onto one knee, the light from overhead twinkling in my face. "Claire, would you do me the great honor of allowing me to be your husband?" Opening up the small black case, I finish my speech.

"Will you marry me?"

I've given her a choice numerous times before, and each one, I thought the uncertainty of her response would drive me insane. But it's nothing compared to the fear I feel right now. I know with all of my heart that Claire loves me, but there's still the slightest chance that she might change her mind about being forever hooked to my wagon.

Claire cups her hands over her mouth, tears springing from her eyes. She bobs her head up and down, her brown waves dangling along her bare shoulders.

My heart nearly jumps out of my chest.

"Is that a yes?" I fight to hide my excitement.

She reaches down to grip onto my face, pulling me up to her. "Yes, a million times over, yes." Claire presses her lips to mine, smiling and laughing and kissing me all at once. "Of course, I'll marry you. Are you really second-guessing that?"

I wrap my arm around her waist, picking her up and spinning her in a circle. I gently lower her to the ground, the petals dancing near us. Sliding the ring out of the box and onto her finger, I didn't think it was possible to be any happier than I already was, but each day with Claire only continues to remind me that even in the darkest of times, if you look for it, there is light.

Claire, my sweet and destructive angel, you are mine.

ACKNOWLEDGMENTS

Every book I write, I seem to go on a journey with my characters. One of growth and change and evolution. I shed layers of myself and uncover parts of me I didn't know existed. This one was no different. It was an absolute honor to tell the beautiful and broken story of Johnny and Claire, and I am thrilled that you came along with us.

To every single person that helped and cheered me on, I thank you immensely. Tiny human. My parents. Vivi. Kate. Sam. Michelle. Clayton. James. Tyler. Victoria. All the ladies behind the street/review teams.

And most of all, my readers. Thank you for believing in me.

ALSO BY TESSA JAMES

Sinners and Angels Duet

Tortured Sinner

Fallen Angel

Untamed Vixen — a dark mafia reverse harem standalone romance set in the *Sinners and Angels* world, following the events of *Fallen Angel*.

BLURB:

I am wild. I am free. And I will not be tamed.

I don't do relationships. I stick around long enough to have a little fun, and then leave before I can be left.

It's not like anyone has ever held my interest very long anyway.

Not until three delectable, mysterious, and frustratingly persistent men show up in my life and completely throw it off course.

It was only supposed to be a one-time thing with each of them, but no matter how hard I try to stay away, we keep getting thrown together.

Before them, everything was mundane. The typical college, work, party, occasional random hookup experience—rinse, repeat. But now, I'm unwillingly thrown into a world of chaos and danger. And if I'm being honest, I love the thrill of it.

The second their rivals catch wind of me, I become a pawn in the twisted war they're in and if I'm not careful, I will end up being just another of the many casualties in this battle of claiming the throne.

Available now... Untamed Vixen

ABOUT THE AUTHOR

Tessa James is the author of dark contemporary romance. She adores writing broken characters you won't help but fall for on their journey to find themselves and fight for what they love. Her stories are for the hopelessly romantic who enjoy grit, angst, and passion.

When she's not writing, you'll find her consuming way too much coffee, making endless to-do lists, and spending time with her daughter and cats in small-town Ohio.

Find Tessa on:
    Tessa James Readers (FB Group)
    Goodreads
    www.tessajamesauthor.com

If you enjoyed reading Johnny & Claire's story, please consider leaving an honest review on Amazon, Goodreads, and/or BookBub.

www.ingramcontent.com/pod-product-compliance
Lightning Source LLC
LaVergne TN
LVHW041627060526
838200LV00040B/1470